SIERRA
GOLD FEVER

SIERRA
GOLD FEVER

D. MICHAEL O'HAVER

AMBASSADOR INTERNATIONAL
GREENVILLE, SOUTH CAROLINA & BELFAST, NORTHERN IRELAND

www.ambassador-international.com

SIERRA GOLD FEVER

©2022 by D. Michael O'Haver

ISBN: 978-1-64960-349-4
eISBN: 978-1-64960-366-1
Library of Congress Control Number: 2022948445

Editing by Katie Cruice Smith
Cover design by Hannah Linder Designs
Interior typesetting by Dentelle Design
Interior illustrations by D. Michael O'Haver

This is a work of fiction. Names, characters, and incidents are all products of the author's imagination or are used for fictional purposes. Any resemblance to actual events or persons, living or dead, is entirely coincidental. Any mentioned brand names, places, and trademarks remain the property of their respective owners, bear no association with the author or the publisher, and are used for fictional purposes only.

AMBASSADOR INTERNATIONAL
Emerald House
411 University Ridge, Suite B14
Greenville, SC 29601
United States
www.ambassador-international.com

AMBASSADOR BOOKS
The Mount
2 Woodstock Link
Belfast, BT6 8DD
Northern Ireland, United Kingdom
www.ambassadormedia.co.uk

The colophon is a trademark of Ambassador, a Christian publishing company.

DEDICATION

This book is dedicated to the original members of the Historical Fiction Spin-off Critique Group at Gold Country Writers in Auburn, California. This is my first venture into this genre, and the formation of this particular critique group was just at the right time, when I thought I was finished with my book. They taught me that there is finished, but not edited. Thank you, Kathleen Ward, Kathy Scogna, and Frank Nissen. You all were invaluable in the final outcome of this exciting venture. I learned more from your critiques about real fiction writing than I had my previous thirty-eight years of professional technical writing experience.

ACKNOWLEDGMENTS

I would like to thank several people for their help and expertise in the writing of this book. First of all, Susan Howland Thompson, Infant Mental Health Specialist and Children's Behaviorist Extraordinaire—I never would have gotten the children's behavior right without you. Thank you also, Chery Anderson, Lenore Brashear, and all the other members of Gold Country Writers who loaned me their reference books on the Old West, the goldfield, and wagon train routes to California. Your advice that went along with the books may have necessitated rewrites on my part, but they also made the story more believable and realistic. I would also like to acknowledge two wonderful beta readers whose suggestions for improvement to the final draft of *Sierra Gold Fever* were invaluable. Thank you, Betsy Schwarzentraub and Janet Ann Collins.

The characters in this novel are imaginary with the exception of the historical figures of Joseph Walker, Samuel Clemens (Mark Twain), Captain Oliver, George McKnight, George D. Roberts, Carmen Knight, James Doty, Chief Wemah, Joaquin Murrieta (Zorro), and Jules Roussiere. All of these people were living during 1853. They were all researched thoroughly. Pease grant me some poetic license in my interpretation of how they would act in my imaginary scenarios.

MAP OF THE RIKER WAGON TRAIN ROUTE TO CALIFORNIA

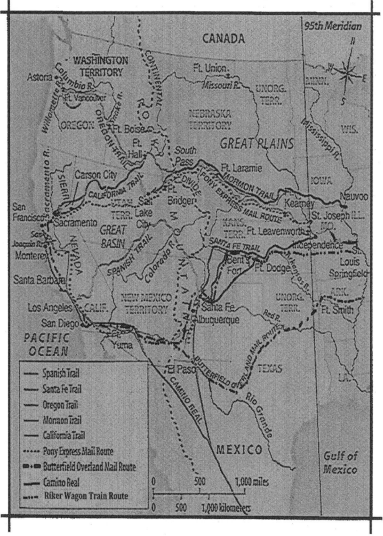

Chapter One

TROUBLE IN THE GOLDFIELD

GRASS VALLEY GOLDFIELD, CALIFORNIA

JUNE 1, 1853

As Jason Miller came out of his thrown-together, temporary shelter built on the banks of Wolf Creek, he glanced at the tintype photograph of Elizabeth, his fiancée, sitting on the packing crate by the door. He gazed at it longingly for a moment but didn't tarry long. He grabbed his gold pan, and as he stepped outside, he immediately encountered Peter Sphenson, his Swedish neighbor on the adjoining claim. He noticed Peter was not heading toward his placer mining claim on Wolf Creek; he was, in fact, heading in the opposite direction.

"Morning, Peter," Jason said in greeting, adjusting his grip on his gold pan. "Have you decided to explore that old, abandoned Bloomfield Mine?"

"Ja," Peter responded, nodding his unruly mop of hair. "I tink I will give it a try; I'm tired of panning for gold all day in a freezing stream. I tink I'll try my luck at hard rock mining."

Jason stopped in front of Peter, momentarily blocking his way. "I still say that old mine is too dangerous. You are going to reinforce the old shoring timbers as you go, right?"

"I will when I get a chance to cut some trees to use. I feel I'm going to hit a big vein," the slightly older man said with a wry smile as he stepped around Jason. Peter readjusted his grip on his pick and shovel and continued on his way toward the old, abandoned mine entrance.

Jason shook his head with exasperation. "Come on, Peter! I really think you should stick to placer mining, panning for the gold like me. It's much safer than that old mineshaft."

Jason stumbled over a stick horse that was a favorite toy of both of Peter's kids. Peter had already started his family. Changing the subject, Jason asked, "Who is watching your kids today?"

Peter turned back slightly to respond, "I got Chin Lee to keep an eye on dem. He is feeling poorly and can't work his laundry."

Peter's wife Mary had taken sick toward the end of their journey to the goldfields with a bad case of whooping cough. She died shortly after arriving, leaving their two kids for her husband to tend while he looked for gold.

Jason had met the Sphenson family on the trip to California. He had immediately taken a shine to Peter and Mary's two offspring.

He'd helped Peter take care of them when Mary was too weak to even get out of their Conestoga wagon without help.

As Peter walked away, Jason noticed he carried a bundle under his arm, along with a pick and shovel. He wondered what that was all about. "Say, Peter . . ." he started to call out, but the miner ducked under the sagging timbers of the old mine entrance, so Jason didn't get a chance to finish asking him.

He shrugged as he went to work, taking his place between other miners stretching out along the nearby Wolf Creek.

Jason was an ambitious but cautious man, unlike Peter, who tended to have the "get rich quick" mentality of so many of the miners. He had learned caution from his foster parents, who had raised him from the age of ten. His natural parents and all his siblings had been killed in a fire that had started from a candle left burning all night. Jason recalled the terror of that night and how he had only escaped by being the closest to the window, which he had liked to keep open at night.

Jason was a man of average build with dark brown hair and brown eyes. After the hours he'd spent standing in ice cold running water, dipping up sand and sediment from the stream bed and swishing the pan around to separate the gold, he was toughened by the rigorous routine. But he'd found it was not an easy way to get rich.

His thoughts turned to his fiancée as he stepped into the cold, rushing waters of Wolf Creek. *I promised Elizabeth I would only be a miner as long as it took me to get us a stake for a good start in our life together, but the way things look, it might take a year or more.*

After about a half-hour panning in Wolf Creek, a loud explosion sounded from the old Bloomfield Mineshaft. Black smoke and dust erupted from the entrance. Jason caught the pungent smell of blasting powder and knew what had been in Peter's mysterious package. He rushed to the mine in alarm, stumbling up the bank of the creek to the mine entrance, only to be blocked from entering by rocks and debris. Jason fanned the air so he could see better and took a moment to get his pounding heartrate down as he assessed what to do next.

Chin Lee arrived with Peter's children. He was so excited, he was speaking his native Mandarin.

"Chin Lee, calm down and speak English," Jason admonished him. "What are you trying to tell me?"

"Peter no listen when I tell him how to use the boom-boom powder," Chin Lee replied, waving his arms in excitement. He started digging with his hands, pulling chunks of rock and dirt from the mine entrance. His panicked state did little to help calm the fears of his two small charges.

Greta yelled in excitement, "What happened? Where's Pappy?"

Greta had just turned ten. Her eight-year-old brother, Sven, was crying. Jason took hold of him and, deciding the boy needed something useful to distract him, said, "Sven, run to Boston Ravine to Jules Roussiere's store and tell him to ring the alarm."

Turning to Greta, he said, "Your pappy is in there, so stay clear and let me help find him."

Sven took off quickly to sound the alarm. Jason started frantically trying to dig out the caved-in mine while still keeping an eye on Greta, who was hysterically crying as well. He was also directing more help as it arrived from the nearby mining claims. He choked on the thick black smoke and dust that was still coming from the caved-in mine entrance. Some of the rescue workers had their picks and shovels from their mining claims, so Jason put them to work digging out the rocks and debris that blocked the mine entrance.

Jason surmised in Peter's haste to strike it rich, he'd obtained some blasting powder from Chin Lee. Being inexperienced in its use, he had blown up the shaft—and most likely himself in the bargain.

They all worked to clear the mine entrance, and Jason led the efforts. Jason had just managed to dig a tunnel into the rubble. In his haste, he wasn't watching the loose rocks above him.

Chin Lee had just uncovered a denim-clad leg and boot, and he called out to Jason about what he had found. Suddenly, a large boulder above Jason slipped and fell.

The last thing Jason heard was a worker behind him yelling, "Watch out!"

But it was too late. The boulder clipped Jason's head, and he slipped into darkness as it landed directly on his right arm.

The relief workers behind Jason quickly came to his assistance, and together, they managed to roll the boulder off Jason and bring him out and away from the mine entrance. Just then, the rocks clogging the mine entrance shifted again, blocking it even worse than before.

Marcos Wilson, who'd been on his way to tend a sick miner but had stopped to help in the rescue efforts, stepped up and said, "Let me look at him. I've had some doctoring experience."

Jason was unconscious, and it didn't take Marcos long to ascertain that Jason's arm was injured beyond repair. He saw that the arm from the elbow on down had been crushed by the boulder. He shook his head in exasperation once again as he lamented the limited medical equipment available in the mining camp. A collective groan went up from the other distraught miners as Marcos exclaimed, "It's injured too badly. I'll have to amputate."

Long John, who was one of the miners helping to move Jason, gasped at Marcos' diagnosis. "Can you do that safely here, Marcos? Do you need any help?"

Marcos directed the miners to a sturdy table made by placing wooden planks over several tree stumps. He cleared the table of the remains from that morning's breakfast to make room for the injured patient. "Yes, I can perform the amputation," he stated. "It is best done as soon as possible. And yes, I can use you, Long John, and a couple others to hold Jason down in case he wakes up will I'm operating. Someone, stoke up that fire. I'll need it to cauterize the wound. Long John, find me the largest knife you can locate."

Long John returned shortly with an old cavalry officer's saber and asked, "Will this do?"

"It will have to do. Here, someone help me out and sharpen that blade up some."

"What if he comes to while you are operating?" another miner asked.

"Well, I don't have any of that newfangled ether they've been using for operations, so he'll just have to bear the pain if he wakes up."

In an aside to Long John, Marcos confided, "I'm not completely sold on ether because I can't depend on the quality of the product. It's so new, there aren't any standards for its manufacture as yet."

When preparations were complete, Marcos instructed, "Now, hold him down tightly . . . and a little prayer won't hurt." He took the sharpened saber in his hands and said a prayer of his own.

Chapter Two

DECISIONS TO MAKE

DAVENPORT, IOWA

JUNE 1, 1853

Elizabeth Dedmore stood on the bank of the Mississippi River. She was supposed to meet her younger brother, Bill, who should have been there a half hour ago. The unique smell of the river, like wet mud, tickled her nose. The late afternoon sunlight sparkled off the water, and the chug, chug, chug of the tugboats pushing barges upstream carried over the cries of the gulls swooping over the river.

Finally, Bill came dragging in. "Where have you been, Billy?" The sounds of the Mississippi almost drowned out her words. "Billy, why can't I depend on you?"

Ignoring his sister's seemingly rhetorical question, Bill pointed to a construction site that was just being set up on the riverbank and asked, "Do you know what they are building down there?"

"I don't have the slightest idea," Elizabeth responded rather sharply. "They're building the first railroad bridge across the river to Rock Island, Illinois."

Bill paced back and forth on the bank. He was seventeen and five years younger than his sister but already three inches taller with a husky build, brown hair, and blue eyes, so he seemed older. Elizabeth was five-foot-six-inches tall, slender, with long, brown hair and blue eyes.

"Lizzy, I was talking to the foreman of that construction crew. That's why I'm a little late."

"Why didn't I know it had something to do with building a bridge and nothing to do with your job at the store? Aren't you supposed to be working on year-end inventory?"

"Boring! I hate inventory. I've finished school, and I'm never going to like working in the family business. I'm going crazy just working at Father's store. He has me learning how to keep the books. I've got no head for 'ciphering. He thinks I'm going to fit in and take over the business someday, but, the truth is, I hate working there. I like the woods, open range, working on construction projects . . . and I love exploring. I've always wanted to go west, and the gold strike in California is my chance to make my fortune my way. I am sick of being told what I'm going to do with my life. Maybe if I'm not reliable doing what they want, they'll let me do what I want."

"I don't know about that, Billy; that's no way to get Mother and Father to agree to let you go to California with me."

Bill jutted out his jaw in that stubborn way he had. "And how are you planning to get them to let you go?"

"I'm working on that," Elizabeth replied with a shrug of her slender shoulders. Unlike most women her age, Elizabeth had an independent streak and was willing to take a gamble to get what her heart desired.

She watched a sternwheeler riverboat hauling bales of cotton steaming upriver past them. Another steamboat passed heading downriver. "I wish I could just jump onto that riverboat and be on my way. I miss Jason so," she said and sighed.

"Well, we could work on it together. They'll never let you go alone, unchaperoned, and I'm the perfect solution. I'll be your chaperone," Bill declared with a grin.

"You have a good point there. Let me think about it." She tugged her left ear, as she did whenever she pondered something important. "Maybe it'll work out for you to go, too, after all. It's been over a year since Jason left for California, and his letters aren't nearly enough to satisfy me."

"What were you going to do about your teaching job? Aren't you planning on teaching next year?" Bill asked, stopping in front of her.

"I've already given the school board my notice," Elizabeth stated with determination. "School is out for the summer, and now is the perfect time for me to go west and meet up with Jason so we can get married." A wistful look came into her eyes as she let her mind wander to the life she planned with Jason. Maybe his promise of someday would be soon.

Sometime later, Elizabeth sat in her favorite daydreaming place—the bay window overlooking the backyard. She gazed up from the letter she was writing Jason at the grand, old maple tree, spreading its limbs far and wide. The green leaves on the tree fluttered as a wind stirred them into life.

Her stout mother came up behind her. "A penny for your thoughts, Lizzy?" She put her short arms as far around Elizabeth as they would reach.

"I really miss Jason; I wish we'd gotten married before he left for California," Elizabeth said as she returned her mother's embrace.

"Jason insisted on being able to support you in the style you're accustomed to."

"I know, but I don't really need all this to make me happy," she replied, releasing her mother's embrace and pointing to the fine cherrywood hutch and loveseat with one hand and out the window at the carriage house flanking the backyard with the other.

"You know, if you get married," her mother said, glancing out the window over her shoulder, "you won't be able to keep your teaching job, and you know how much you love teaching those kids."

"I am a little torn, and I know that may be true here in Iowa; but I've heard out west, where there's so few women, they let mothers teach school. Jason and I have talked, and we want lots of children. I'm real anxious to get started with my own family."

"I can't stand to think of you moving away, but I suppose it's inevitable. I know you want to make your own life."

Now's as good a time as ever. "It may be sooner than you think. I'm considering going out to California and joining Jason."

"You can't be serious!" Her mother reacted with amazement, placing her fists on her hips as she did when asserting her authority. "Why, you've never been outside of Iowa—and to Des Moines only twice. How would you travel there, and who would chaperone you? It just wouldn't be proper for you to travel on your own."

"I'll go by wagon train. I've checked on the cost, and I have enough saved up from my teaching salary to pay for it myself. It's only a two-day journey down the Mississippi River to St. Louis, where I can join a wagon train heading west."

Elizabeth's mother plopped herself down on the window seat next to her and said, "Why would you want to go by wagon train? Don't they have stagecoaches that go all the way to California?"

"Yes, they do; but the cost is too much, and they only allow you twenty-five pounds of luggage. I can travel light, but not that light. If I had an address in California, I could ship some of my things, but Jason doesn't have a real address yet."

"You still haven't answered my question about your chaperone, young lady."

"Bill could go with me as my chaperone, Mother."

"You have got to be kidding!" She shot to her feet. "He can barely take care of himself, let alone you. We'll see what your father has to say about all this." With that, Elizabeth's mother twirled around and stomped off.

Later that evening after dinner, Elizabeth learned just what her father had to say. "Absolutely not! I'll not have any daughter of mine gallivanting across the country! And on a wagon train?" In his excitement, he dropped the pouch of tobacco he was filling his after-dinner pipe with onto his lap. "Don't you remember what happened to the Donner Party back in '47? They were trapped in the Sierra Mountains and snowed in and ran out of food. Some reports say they resorted to cannibalism to survive."

He brushed the spilled tobacco off his lap and started filling his pipe all over again. "And what were you planning to do about a chaperone for the journey?"

Mother cut in. "Wait until you hear this, dear."

"Well . . . I haven't really planned that out yet." Elizabeth hesitated, unsure of herself. "But what would you say if Bill went with me and was my chaperone?"

"What! That's preposterous!" he blustered. "Bill is going to carry on with the Dedmore Mercantile when I'm ready to retire. He hasn't said anything to me about going west."

"That's because he didn't want to disappoint you. He feels bad about letting you and the family down by not taking over and running the store."

"You never answered me about the dangers of the trip out west."

Elizabeth's mother tried to intervene. "Charles, please! Let's hear her out."

"But, Father, I'm not planning on taking that route. I've been reading about a southern route that goes through Missouri and Arkansas to Fort Dodge. From there, I would go south through Santa Fe and take the Southern Overland Trail to Los Angeles. There's no snow or mountains that way. Then we'll go up the California coast to the goldfields above Sacramento."

"You're showing some of your mother's common sense, at least." Her father's expression changed to one of tolerance toward his willful daughter. "I have business friends in Santa Fe who will be happy to help you if you get that far. What were you planning on doing once you get there? Has Jason even gotten established yet? It's been only a year."

"The last letter I received said he was still prospecting for gold. But that doesn't mean Jason and I couldn't get married. And I could teach school."

"What do you mean, you could teach school? Married women can't teach school."

"That's not so out west; there are so few women, they let married women teach."

Father got up from his easy chair and restlessly stomped around the den, clenching his pipe. Mother dropped into her chair and fanned herself with her apron.

Elizabeth went to bed that night, leaving the Dedmore household still in upheaval.

While Elizabeth and Bill were trying to convince their parents, they were grown up enough to travel to California on their own, on a farm a few hundred miles away, just outside a little town in Arkansas, Bob Sterling's wife, Betsy, had been fighting a bad case of yellow fever.

Dr. White came out of the Sterling bedroom with a despondent look. His drooping mustache covered the grim set to his lips, but his downcast eyes didn't meet Bob Sterling's.

Bob jumped to his feet to confront the doctor. "How is Betsy?" he asked.

The doctor's voice was very sad and tired. "I'm afraid she just passed away."

Bob staggered a little, then caught himself with a hand on the fireplace mantel. "What will Esther do now without a mother?"

Esther, who was only six, just plopped down into a chair and sat there with a vacant stare.

Bob was afraid of how Esther would cope with this tragedy. Esther was so fragile and did not have many friends her age to help her through such a trauma.

Betsy's funeral was a few days later, and Esther were still in shock. With downcast eyes, Bob stood solemnly in his best dark wool suit. Pastor Evert shook Bob's hand and offered his condolences. "I'm so sorry, Bob, for your loss. What will you do now?"

"I'm thinking about selling everything and heading west for a fresh start."

Meanwhile in a nearby town, another family was contemplating moving west as well.

"I hope you're proud of yourself, Steward," Mother said with her hands on her hips. "It's disgraceful what you did to that girl, Julie. What do you have to say for yourself?" She ruled this household, and everyone knew it.

"Steward," his father angrily chimed in, berating his son, which was something he seldom did. "Thanks to the trouble you've gotten yourself into, we are going to have to sell out and move west."

Steward was outraged. His face got beat red, and he stomped across the room, stopping in front of his father. "You can't do this to me. What if I don't want to go west? I'm of age. I can do what I want, and you can't make me go."

Steward's parents gaped in astonishment, with their mouths hanging open, as their son slammed out of the house.

Chapter Three

COMING TO GRIPS

GRASS VALLEY GOLDFIELD, CALIFORNIA

JUNE 12, 1853

Jason woke up to the sound of faraway voices. It seemed like he was deep down in a well. Gradually, the voices got louder as if he was floating to the top. When he could make sense through the haze, he could tell the voices were arguing about who was going to take care of Sven and Greta, who were now orphans. He couldn't quite make out who was talking at first.

"Well, I don't have time to watch over those kids and work my claim at the same time."

Another voice responded, "Well, neither do any of us, so what're we gonna do?"

Jason responded in a weak voice, "I take it Peter didn't make it. I promised him that I'd take care of the kids if anything happened to him."

"Well, look who's back with the living. You're not in any shape to be taking care of anyone right about now," responded Marcos, who was hovering nearby.

Marcos Wilson had decided to try his luck in the Northern California goldfield. He had been discharged from the army at Fort Rosecrans near San Diego, California. But he soon found he spent more time doctoring the medically deprived miners than he did actually mining. He provided medical services, often without pay, to those in need just because he couldn't stand by when such services were needed. He figured God gave him the skills to heal the injured, and it would be dishonoring God if he didn't use those skills when needed.

Jason found himself on a cot outdoors by the campfire. He tried moving his arms. His left arm responded properly, but there was something wrong with his right arm. When he could finally focus, he was horrified to see that his right shirt sleeve ended in . . . .nothing. Jason broke down in sobs with the realization that his right arm now ended shortly below his elbow.

As he was beginning to feel the darkness closing in again, Jason heard Marcos say, "He should be out for quite some time with the amount of laudanum I gave him for his pain. I wish there was more I could do for him."

Please, Lord, give me the strength to survive.

###

Several of the other miners who had tried to help dig out the mine cave-in stood around the campfire discussing the incident. "That cave-in yesterday at the Bloomfield Mine just goes to show how it's way too dangerous in those hard rock mine shafts," exclaimed Long John, as he combed his whiskers with his corncob pipe. "Us private miners just don't have the equipment needed to mine that-a-way. It takes timbers to shore up the shaft and drills to dig to the vein, and if you've got in far enough, you need rails and cars to get the ore out. It's better to stick to panning or using rockers, long toms, ground sluices, and sluice boxes."

"That's why all those mining companies are being formed. They can afford all that fancy mining equipment," Mike, a tall, gangly former deckhand from a clipper ship now sitting abandoned in San Francisco harbor, noted.

"The time for us individual miners making it here in the California goldfield on our own is almost over," replied Long John.

"Where did Peter get the blasting powder, anyway?" asked Stephen. He threw a log onto the fire. Stephen was in Grass Valley to strike it rich, and he didn't care much how he did it. His claim wasn't paying off, and he was looking for a way out; but he wanted a stake before he left.

"How did he afford to buy it? It must have cost a fortune," another man asked.

"He didn't get it at Roussiere's store, I'll bet. The prices there are jacked up so high, no one could afford them," complained Stephen.

"Roussiere doesn't jack up his prices as much as Brannan did at his store at Fort Sutter back in '49. I had to pay sixteen dollars for a twenty-cent gold pan," replied another. "Anyone who opens a store in the goldfield has a captive audience. No one wants to take time out to go to the nearest town for supplies when he could spend it finding gold."

"I hear he got it from the Chinaman, Chin Lee," Joe Preston replied.

"Yeah, but how did Peter pay for it? Does the Chinaman take gold dust?" Stephen asked.

"Of course, he does. He's not stupid," replied Mike.

"I wonder where Peter's stash is. Does anyone know?" Stephen asked.

"No, but maybe one of his kids does. We'll have to ask them," Joe replied.

"So, what's gonna happen to the Swede's kids?" Mike asked. "Jason is not going to be able to tend them for quite some time."

"I think we should all take turns until Jason gets well enough to take over," Long John proposed.

###

While the independent miners were deciding the fate of the newly orphaned kids, George McKnight and Jim Buchanan, his righthand man, stood talking a half-mile up and on the other side of the South fork of Wolf Creek from where the miners were.

"With the men we lost in that last cave-in of my mine, we need more men to work that new vein," stated McKnight. "Is that group of placer miners still working their claims further down on Wolf Creek?"

They stood on the hillside next to the Gold Hill Quartz Mine entrance. Wolf Creek's rushing waters behind them nearly drowned out their voices.

Buchanan raised his voice to be heard. "Yes, Boss, but they are stubborn. They've got something against hard rock mining."

"When I first came to Grass Valley—it was called Boston Ravine then—I worked Wolf Creek, but everyone should know it's worked out by now. I found where the real strike is on Gold Hill. They should be happy to come work for me. I'll pay them a decent wage, and they won't have to spend all day freezing to death in that infernal creek. I hope I've made myself clear. I want you to go to work on them. Find someone in their group that we can use."

"Yes, Boss."

Later, Buchanan stood outside a large miner's cabin that was known to house several of the independent miners. He approached Stephen and another miner named Luke. He had heard that they were open to recruitment.

"We need help persuading that group of independent miners that they need to come to work for us at Gold Hill."

"What's in it for us?" Luke asked.

"We could either give you good jobs as foremen, or we could discuss payments in gold for each recruit you provide."

Stephen replied, "I'd prefer the gold."

Luke chimed in, "Me, too."

"Great, now it all depends on how fast you can get them to sign up with us. If you could get some of those miners to come to work for McKnight, he'd pay you twenty-five dollars a head. But you must get them to sign up within a week. Get to work and report back to me."

Buchanan rubbed his hands together, satisfied he'd found a way to replace the five men they'd lost recently in the mine cave-in.

Jason awoke after another restless night's sleep. His memory was fuzzy about when he awoke after the mine accident. He felt apprehensive, like there was something terrible that had happened. All of the sudden, he remembered what it was—he was a cripple. He was embarrassed that he'd broken down and succumbed to tears. The thought that penetrated the pain was, *What will Lizzy think of me now?*

Marcos knocked on Jason's flimsy door.

"Come in," Jason responded.

Marcos, who was there to tend to Jason's arm, ducked into the small shelter and said, "How are you feeling, Jason? Has the drug I gave you for the pain worn off yet?"

"The pain isn't too bad." *Just bad enough to remind me of what I lost.* "How would you feel if you lost your right arm?" Jason continued bitterly.

Marcos winced in guilt but responded, "I had no other choice but to amputate. Your injury was too bad. Another few inches the wrong way and you'd be dead, crushed by that boulder. You should be thanking the good Lord above that you survived."

It was Jason's turn to wince in guilt. "I know; I know. But how do you expect me to survive? I'm righthanded—or I was before . . . " His voice trailed off.

"I'm willing to work with you and teach you how to use your left hand. If you practice enough, you'll soon be able to use your left hand as good as you did your right."

There was no response from Jason, who was sulking. When he sulked, he didn't want company. He just wanted solitude.

"But for now, let me look at that arm. I need to make sure you aren't getting an infection." Marcos gently took Jason's arm and unwrapped the bandage covering it. He was pleased to see it was healing nicely.

How can a one-armed miner expect to make his fortune in the California goldfields? If I hadn't promised to take care of the Swede's kids, I'd pack it in and give up right now. Why did You let this happen, Lord?

Marcos, who was dressed this morning in trousers from his old army uniform and a plaid flannel shirt, common among the miners, decided to change the subject. "What do your folks think about your accident?"

"I haven't told my foster family anything yet."

"So, what happened to your natural parents?"

"They were killed in a fire when I was only ten."

"Where are your foster parents?"

"They live in Iowa."

"Did you have any foster brothers or sisters?"

"No, that is why I was adopted. My foster parents couldn't have any kids on their own. I'll have to write them soon to let them know about the accident and how I'm doing."

Jason was done with the visit. Turning his back on his friend, he pretended to fall asleep until he heard the doctor quietly shut the door behind him.

###

Jason gradually improved and in a week's time was able to get up and move about without assistance. One day, Long John was visiting with Jason. The two men were sitting on an old oak log in the oak and pine woodland near Grass Valley. A jackrabbit scampered across their path and disappeared into the undergrowth. A woodpecker pecked away on a dead oak tree off to their left. The sun's warming rays slanted through the overhead tree branches.

Jason was not acting like himself. He slumped over with his elbows on his knees, staring at the pine needles and oak leaves under his feet. He didn't seem to notice anything that went on around him. Long John was worried about the change in Jason since the accident. His concern centered around how depressed Jason seemed now and his loss of faith. He'd found he liked the younger man and greatly respected his commitment to getting a stake for his upcoming marriage.

"What will it take to lift your spirits?" he asked Jason.

Jason replied, "You're always talking about God. Tell me, why would God let me lose my right hand when He knows I need it to do a miner's job?"

"I don't know, Son. Maybe you're not meant to be a miner. We don't always know God's true plans for us."

"I've always believed in God and trusted Him to take care of me. Why is He letting me down now?"

"God never promised that we'll not have adversity in our lives. He just said He'd be with us and guide us through it."

"I've always felt close to God, even in times of trouble. Why do I feel like He has gone away somewhere and left me all alone this time?"

"I've found that when that happens, it's usually us who have gone away from God, not the other way around."

Long John was aware he was neglecting his mining claim to spend time trying to lift Jason's spirits. He didn't mind so much; he was quite fond of the young miner. Long John, like many of the miners working Wolf Creek, was a relative newcomer to the California Goldfield. He'd arrived three years ago. He managed to make enough to live on but not enough to call it a strike. Being older than the other miners, he'd assumed the role of mentor or father, especially to Jason.

He knew Jason was hurting, and he would do everything in his power to lead the young man back to God.

Later that night, Jason sat at the campfire along with Marcos and practiced eating with his left hand. His spoon wobbled terribly as he brought it to his mouth. At the last moment, the contents fell off into his lap. He muttered some choice words under his breath before exclaiming, "This accident has really slowed me down." He threw his spoon down in frustration. He dumped the rest of the stew that was in his bowl directly into his mouth instead.

"You'll never learn unless you practice. Keep at it, and it will get easier," Marcos admonished him.

"I'll never make it as a miner with just a left hand." Jason stared glumly into the dark shadows, which flickered as the fire flared up, then died down again. "I've got quite a lot of gold dust stored up for my and Elizabeth's stake, but not nearly as much as I intended to get before I quit."

Changing the subject, Jason asked, "How are the Swede's kids doing, anyway? I feel guilty after promising him I'd take care of them if anything happened to him."

"They're getting by. They miss their father, of course. Long John said Sven hasn't talked since his father died. Long John has organized some of the miners to pitch in and take turns minding the kids until you're ready to take over."

Jason sighed and shook his head in frustration. "I don't know how soon that will be. I can't even feed myself, let alone take care of two kids." Jason flapped the stump of his right arm. He was so discouraged at his misfortune that he felt like an invalid without any hope.

"Your arm is healing nicely. It won't be long until you're fully healed. Adam has offered to carve you a fake hand out of pine wood. Have you seen those? They look almost like the real thing when they're painted the right way. I'll fit it to your arm when it's all healed up."

"Who's Adam?"

"He's the eighteen-year-old son of Joe Preston. They're working that claim over on Squirrel Creek."

"Well, at least I will look like a complete man again," said Jason bitterly. But inwardly, his anger just grew as he mourned the loss of his dreams.

Stephen was working his mining claim, sort of. He'd set it aside to go with his offer from Gold Hill. He lived in a cabin with six other miners. He was breaking in a new partner named Melvin. They worked together, mining with a long tom.

Melvin asked, "How does this contraption work?"

"Well, you see this long trough? We made it about eight feet long, some eighteen inches wide, and about six inches high. There's an iron sieve in one end punched with half-inch holes. Underneath this, we placed a box with two ripples or raised areas across it."

"Why is it positioned at this angle to the stream?"

"How should I know? That's just the way Bart and Lefty set it up. We run water through it with this hose. You throw the gravel from the stream in and stir it with a shovel until the water runs clear. The gold and finer gravel drop through the sieve and fall into the box down under and lodge above the ripples. The water running through the long tom washes over the loose gravel, and all the gold, being heavier, settles to the bottom. One man can wash as fast as two can pick and shovel it in."

Stephen was a hard worker when anyone was watching. But he was thinking about the easy money Buchanan had offered for recruiting workers for McKnight's hard rock mine. The cabin where he lived was located near their claim on Wolf Creek. Luke, who also lived in the cabin, was a lazy slacker. He came out and watched Stephen and Melvin working the long tom. He was dressed in baggy, denim pants, which hadn't seen a cleaning in over a week, and a patched flannel shirt, equally as filthy. His cabinmates were constantly after him to do his share of the work. He often as not ran off to do who-knew-what just to get out of work.

When Stephen and Melvin finally took a lunch break, Stephen had a chance to talk to Luke.

Stephen asked, "Did you get a lead on any recruits for McKnight?" Stephen was dressed somewhat better than his friend Luke in canvas pants and a plaid shirt that looked like it had just come from Chin Lee's laundry.

"Na, I fell asleep early and didn't get no chance. I'll try again tonight."

Stephen changed the subject and, lowering his voice to a conspiratorial level, said, "We have to find where the Swede stashed all his gold. The way I figure it, finders keepers."

"I'm with you on that," Luke replied.

"Let's head over to the assay office and see who's filing new claims."

The next morning, instead of working their mining claim, Stephen had joined up with his cohort, Luke, and they searched for Peter Sphenson's gold stash. They'd heard it was common practice for miners to often hide their accumulated gold somewhere in or close to their claim or living structure. Most miners didn't want to take the time away from panning to go into town where there were banks. So, Stephen and Luke were searching in the woods surrounding the Swede's cabin.

After spending several fruitless hours, Stephen commented, "We'll never find it at this rate. The Swede could have stashed it anywhere. We're just wasting our time. We should be trying to recruit miners for McKnight." He kicked a pinecone away in disgust. It bounced off a rock and landed by an oak tree.

Luke replied, "We need to search the cabin he was living in; that's the most likely place." Luke was as unscrupulous as Stephen. He would do just about anything to get a stake, whether it was rightfully his or not.

"I guess you're right. Let's do it now, while the kids are over at Preston's place. It's his turn to watch them today."

A short time later, the two miners, now turned thieves, had ripped up the sleeping pallets and pillows at the Swede's cabin. It was not much bigger than Jason's shanty next door but had originally housed a family of four. Feathers and stuffing covered the remains of the furniture, which was strewn all over the one-room structure. There was no indication of anyone digging in the dirt floor lately, so they hadn't bothered searching there. They had even overturned the cook stove in the corner and searched it thoroughly.

After tearing the cabin apart with no luck, the two talked together outside under the oak trees with the noontime sun almost directly overhead.

"I still say the kids must know something about where their pappy kept his gold," said Stephen.

"Probably so, but how do we get it out of them?"

"It's my turn to tend them tomorrow; I'll think of something."

"We need to get to work persuading the rest of the miners to go to work for McKnight."

"I know. I plan on bringing it up around the campfire tonight," Stephen replied, as the two made their way back toward their own claims on Wolf Creek.

Changing the subject, Luke said, "We need to find us a big strike so we can get out of this place."

"You mean like George D. Roberts did back in '50?"

"Yeah, but Mr. Roberts is now a down-on-his-luck miner working a claim on Cherry Creek."

"Yeah, but we'll be smart enough to hold on to our claim. I heard that's what started the gold rush to Grass Valley. They say Mr. Roberts found that hard rock mine but mined it only a short time, then sold his claim for a measly $350. Now, they're calling it the Empire Mine. Some say it's the richest hard rock mine in the goldfield. We need us a strike like that."

Greta lectured her little brother Sven in the front yard of their cabin. "You have to get over Pappy's death. Life goes on; we have to find a way to get by."

Greta had acted out her grief at her mother's death by picking fights with her friends, who were just trying to console her in her loss. Now, with the death of her father, Greta saw that she had to be strong for her brother's sake. She had changed somewhat and become more maternal.

Sven was moping around. He had recently started getting over losing his mother. Now his world had been turned upside down again with the death of his father. He didn't say anything to his sister. He simply opened his arms, and Greta quickly took him and held him tightly for a long time. He was a confused little boy who was unsure what the future held.

Chapter Four

THE JOURNEY BEGINS

MISSISSIPPI RIVER NEAR BURLINGTON, IOWA

JUNE 15, 1853

They were slowly passing a giant flotilla of logs being guided downriver to sawmills in Keokuk and Quincy. Between the logs and the riverboat, the *George Washington*, were several flatboats. These were long, narrow, barge-like boats without power that carried cargo such as pork, corn, furs, fruits, vegetables, and whiskey downstream only. The brother and sister had just passed Burlington, so their journey had officially begun.

"Pshaw! This is a bully way to travel. It sure beats traveling by horseback or in our old buckboard," exclaimed Bill. "How did you get

Father to agree and pay for this? When I talked to him, he wasn't very happy that I wanted to go, too."

"It was his idea, actually, once he got used to the fact that we were going, one way or the other. It was harder getting him to accept that you were going than it was that I was going. He knows how much I miss Jason. He went on and on how no kid of his was going to suffer like he did when he moved to Davenport. I'm glad he came around. Now, we can save our money for a better wagon and team."

"Speaking of money, I haven't saved up much from my salary working at the store, but I'm donating what's left to help pay for our trip. I can't wait to get to California and find my share of gold," declared Bill.

"Thank you, Brother."

"I can't get over how the Mississippi has its own unique smell, like wet clay," Elizabeth said, taking a large breath of the humid air.

Captain Oliver, the ship's captain, strolled by and stopped to chat with them. He wore snappy, pressed, and creased trousers and a matching coat with gold buttons with anchors embossed on them. A traditional captain's hat with a shiny black visor completed his attire.

"Is this your first time on a riverboat?"

"Yes, sir. We've lived in Davenport all our lives and watched the riverboats going up and down the Mississippi, but we've never been on one before."

"These sidewheel riverboats sure are a lot easier to steer—and quieter for the passengers, too. Everyone was amazed when Henry Shreve started building them back in 1824. They thought they would be too top heavy with three stories above the water."

"Why is it easier to steer?" Bill asked.

"We can reverse one side paddle and not the other, so we can turn in our own length."

"I would think you'd be more inclined to get caught up on snags with the paddles on the side," Bill said.

"That would be true if we didn't have one of the best pilots on the Mississippi. Woodward is his name. He has an apprentice who's an excellent storyteller. Be sure and come out to the promenade deck this evening and catch him in action."

"Do you carry cargo as well as passengers?" asked Elizabeth.

"We sure do, and our passenger accommodations are bigger and better than most you'll find. The whole first and second-story setback levels are for passengers; cargo is below deck, and the pilothouse is on the third story."

"We like it a lot. And we appreciate you letting us share a cabin," remarked Bill.

"I was happy to accommodate your father. He has given us a lot of business shipping merchandise for his store." With a slight nod, the captain moved on about his business of running a big steamboat.

Later that afternoon in their cabin, Elizabeth pushed back her chair, and it bumped into the bunk built into their stateroom wall.

"Do you think this room could be any smaller?" said Bill with a chuckle.

"Well, at least it's larger than the single cabins they tried to stick us in at first—but not by much." The accommodations consisted of two small bunkbeds built into one wall—one above the other—a small, circular table with two spindly chairs, and room to stack their trunks. There were nails in one wall to hang coats and extra clothes on and one portal for air circulation, and that was it.

"I'll take the upper bunk," Bill declared, throwing his bedroll up on it.

Not much privacy, Elizabeth thought to herself. *But I had better get used to it. The wagon we'll be taking on the rest of the trip will be even smaller and more crowded.*

"How long will the wagon train take to get us to California?" Bill asked his sister.

"It depends on which train we get and which route they're taking. The southernmost route, which is the safest, takes four or five months to get to Los Angeles, and then it's another week's journey up the coast to the goldfields above Sacramento. So, it will be early fall by the time we get there—if we're lucky."

"That's a long time. Isn't there a faster way?" asked Bill.

"There are other shorter routes, but then we would have the Rockies and Sierra Mountains to contend with, and Father forbade us to take one of them. We will try to get a wagon train that's taking the southern route that goes by way of Arkansas, Texas, and the recently purchased New Mexico Territory. Billy, I know you want to hurry up and make your fortune so you can get on with your life."

"How long does it take going by boat around the Horn?" Bill asked.

"It would take up to nine months, unless we got off at Panama and walk across the isthmus, then catch another ship on the other side, which would be too risky for my taste."

"Why is it so risky? It doesn't look any more than fifty miles on the map," Bill exclaimed.

"It's under that—around forty-eight—but there are swamps to cross; that means mosquitoes. Mosquitoes mean malaria. Then there's the bandits who kidnap folks like us and hold them for ransom."

"Okay, you can count me out of that route. You would think that someone would build a railroad across the isthmus."

"Actually, they have started one," Elizabeth confided. "Back in 1850, one was started; but they've run into so many delays, it's not finished yet."

"Oh, I hope there's some gold left by the time we get there," declared the impatient youth.

Elizabeth just laughed. She was used to Bill's impetuous nature.

That evening, Bill and Elizabeth gathered with some of the other passengers on the promenade deck to be entertained. The apprentice river guide by the name of Samuel Clemens told them the tale of *Dick Baker's Cat.*

The story was about a miner named Dick Baker and a remarkable cat by the name of Tom Quartz that he had owned for eight years. This cat was uncanny in his mining intuition. Whenever Dick would try a new location, Tom the cat would either encourage him or, if he deemed the prospects dim, discourage him from continuing. And the remarkable thing was the cat was always right.

Then when hard rock mining became the popular thing, Tom the cat showed without a doubt that he was against it. Naturally, Dick had to try it at least once. So, he found a likely spot, dug himself a shaft, set himself some blasting powder, and lit the fuse, forgetting that Tom was asleep in the corner. Well, when that powder went off,

Tom was blown, along with the rocks and dirt, sky high; and when he came down, he let it be known that quartz mining was too risky and dangerous, and nothing Dick could do or say would dissuade Tom from his opinion.

As the crowd that had gathered on the promenade deck to hear the storyteller dispersed, Bill and Elizabeth had a chance to chat with Mr. Clemens.

"That was some story, Mr. Clemens. Did you write that yourself?" Elizabeth complimented him.

"Why, thank you, ma'am. Yes, I wrote that little story in my spare time. I'm training to be a riverboat pilot."

"What exactly does a riverboat pilot do?" Elizabeth wanted to know.

"I keep the boat from getting caught up on snags, like dead trees and rocks in the river. We have to know just where the channel is deep enough for the boat to travel safely. The river is constantly changing, so we have to keep up on all those changes." He pointed up ahead to a sandbar extending about halfway across the river. "See that sandbar up there? We have to steer clear of it for sure." Another river boat was seen passing them heading upstream close to the sandbar. "That's the *Amenity II*, and it's a sternwheeler." He indicated with an arm wave. "It's got a much shallower draft and can take the chance to get closer to that sandbar than us. Where might you two be traveling to?"

"My sister and I are on our way down river to St. Louis to catch a wagon train to California. I'm going to strike it rich in the goldfields. And my sister, Elizabeth, is joining her fiancé, who's a miner in Grass Valley."

"Bully for you, young man! I wish you the best of luck, and you, too, ma'am. But you remember to stick to placer mining—none of that quartz mining, you hear!"

The next morning, Bill and Elizabeth departed the riverboat in St. Louis. "I'm glad that's over with," exclaimed Bill.

The jumping-off place for wagon trains heading west was bustling. Horses and riders, buckboards, and pedestrians filled the narrow streets. Bill and Elizabeth were lucky to find wooden boardwalks built on some of the streets to get away from the street traffic. They found their way to Bosman's Mercantile Store, recommended by their father, where they started the task of purchasing the supplies they would need for the journey.

"Can I help you folks?" a friendly clerk at the counter asked.

Elizabeth pulled out the list she had made when talking to her father and gave it to the clerk. "Here, start with this." She added, "We'll also need mustard, cinnamon, nutmeg, vinegar, pepper, and any other spices that you like, Billy."

Bill gave the clerk his preferences in spices and a list for clothing for himself for the three months' journey. Then he asked, "What about the weapons and powder needed for the trip? And we'll need extra ammunition for me to practice with."

Elizabeth asked, "What about that rifle you used when you went shooting with Father?"

"I've outgrown that musket. It's time I had my very own rifle."

"We have some of those newfangled Enfield 1853 muskets. Would you like to see one of those?" the clerk asked.

"Yes, sir."

"This is a .577-caliber mini-type, muzzle-loading rifle, which is being used by the British. What about handguns?"

"We already have those, but we'll need extra ammunition."

"We can't forget the tools needed to repair the wagons on the trip," Elizabeth reminded Bill. "We will also need supplies for mending clothes—several spools of stout, linen thread, large needles, beeswax, a few buttons, a paper of pins, a thimble, and a small, cloth bag for all the sewing products."

"What about cooking?" Bill reminded his sister, as he looked around the well-stocked store with shelves loaded with every imaginable item that could be useful on a wagon train heading westward.

"Oh, yes, how could I forget that? The cooking articles and utensils needed, which include a Dutch oven."

Their clerk asked them, "Do you want one of the fancy Revere ovens with the flat lid and ridges on it for heaping coals onto?"

"No, we're on a budget, and that's too costly." Elizabeth wasn't much of a cook, having been raised with servants, which included a cook, but she was practical and knew how to stay on the budget she'd made for the trip west. "We'll pick up our order later when we have a wagon," Elizabeth told the clerk.

They then went to a wagon supplier, who also had a blacksmith who modified custom Conestoga wagons. It was another place recommended by their father.

"We want a modification that involves building into the wagon a secret compartment we can use as a safe box for keeping our money and small valuables." Bill repeated what his father had recommended.

"We also want our wagon caulked for waterproofing," Elizabeth added.

"Yes, ma'am, we can do that, but it will add to the cost and take an extra day."

"That'll be fine."

They went next to the stockyard, where they purchased the oxen they needed to pull the wagon and a horse for Bill to ride when he wasn't driving the wagon.

"Some people prefer draft horses or mules to pull their wagons," the livery man told them.

"What is the difference in price?" asked Elizabeth.

"Oxen are the cheapest, then horses, with mules being the most expensive."

"We'll stick with the oxen," Elizabeth decided. "I hear the natives along the way have no use for oxen. We'll need two good, matched pairs and a spare."

Last of all, they found a hotel to stay the night, where they collapsed in exhaustion after a very busy day.

Early the next morning, Elizabeth and Bill asked directions at their hotel and sought out John Riker, who had been commissioned as captain of the next wagon train leaving for California.

Elizabeth asked, "Mr. Riker, which route are you taking to California?"

"We will take the Santa Fe Trail to Santa Fe. Then I plan on dropping down south to the Southern Overland route. It's being considered for a stagecoach and mail route to California. It's usually too dry to consider this late in the year, but I have just talked to an old friend, a scout of mine who just returned using that route. He assured me there is plenty of water. His name is Joseph Walker, and his only caution is that the Chickasaw are on the uprise in Indian Territory. He'll be the scout for our trip to California. I'm planning on leaving in two days; can you be ready by then?"

Bill answered, "We can be. Where do we meet you?"

"The train is forming up just south of town on the bank of the river by the cottonwood grove. Just ask for the Riker Train; anyone can direct you."

The following day, Elizabeth was talking to a gentleman she had met at breakfast at their hotel—a Mr. Brown. He was a merchant who happened to know their father. She was a little put out that they were not taking the southern route all the way, which bypassed Santa Fe.

She asked, "What do you know about John Riker and his scout, Joseph Walker?"

"I assure you, John Riker is an experienced wagon master, who has taken several wagon trains west over the last fifteen years."

"Why was he able to make trips west but not east?" Elizabeth puzzled.

"He has a business that takes him east several times a year, and he decided to make the best of the journey back to the west. He has traveled most of the various routes to California, including the Overland Trail. He has experienced some bad trips and some good ones. There are close to sixty wagons gathered for this trip, and Riker was heard committing to making this trip one of the best ones."

"And what about Joseph Walker?" Elizabeth asked.

"You've never heard of Joe Walker, the famous mountain man?" Mr. Brown's tone was incredulous.

"Oh, you mean he's *that* Joseph Walker; of course, we've heard of him," Bill cut in, kicking his sister under the table.

Elizabeth gave Bill a look but didn't say any more right then.

Later, back in their hotel room, Bill assured his sister that they were very lucky to have *the* Joseph Walker scouting for their train. "Why, he's been to California many times and explored other parts of the west. He's a famous frontiersman. I'm surprised you've never heard of him."

Bill argued with Elizabeth, "I think we should collect our stuff from the mercantile, wagon maker, and stockyard and spend the night with the wagon train so we'll be ready bright and early to leave for California."

"You sure you don't want one more night of sleeping in a real bed, Billy?"

"Nope," Bill replied. "I'm eager to get on with this adventure. And by the way, don't call me Billy anymore. My name is Bill."

Bill won the argument, and they checked out of the hotel and went to pick up their wagon and stock, loaded all their supplies, and joined the wagon train that very evening.

Around the campfire that night at a gathering of many of the would-be pioneers preparing for the western journey, Elizabeth was captivated by a family of a small, withdrawn girl and her father. She wondered where the mother was. The girl, around six, was dressed in a blue gingham dress and was quite shy around all the strangers. The father was tall, handsome, well-dressed, and polite. His name was Bob Sterling, and Elizabeth found out from the conversation he was a widower, who was going west for a new start after the death of his wife.

Adding another log to the fire, Bill asked, "Mr. Sterling, where do you plan to settle?" Then he and several others backed away from the flare-up of the campfire.

"Well, Young Man, I haven't really decided yet. I've signed on to this train because of the route. I like what I hear about New Mexico and California. I may not go all the way to California, though, if I find a place I really like along the way. I will know more after I see the lay of the land along the way."

Trying to get to know the family, Emily asked, "What is your girl's name?" Elizabeth asked.

"This shy one hiding behind my leg is Esther." Esther peeked around her father's leg with a thumb stuck in her mouth. "You seem to like children. Do you have any children of your own?"

Elizabeth demurred in embarrassment at the too-personal question.

Bill answered for her. "Ha! No! She's not married, but she likes children because she was a school marm."

"That's interesting. I happen to be looking for some way to start my girl's schooling. We probably won't get to where we are going before school is supposed to start, and I don't want her to get behind. And Esther is having some problems that need special attention."

"Oh, what kind of problems, if I might ask?" Elizabeth said.

"She has always been quiet and shy with strangers, but since her mother's death, she has been even more so. Her mother was kind, considerate, and nurturing. She loved Esther and didn't want anything else except to raise her family the best that she could. Esther hardly talks to anyone now, even me. I am starting to get really concerned about her. I would prefer to discuss it further with you in private, if you are interested in taking on the job."

Elizabeth thought to herself, *What a beautiful, complicated child that Esther is. I'm dying to get to know her better. And it would be wonderful to continue teaching while we travel.*

After conversing privately with Mr. Sterling, Elizabeth decided that teaching Esther was just the thing to do to keep their minds off the tediousness of travel. She gathered that Mr. Sterling was a committed family man. He liked married life, but he was a provider, not a nurturer. He loved his little girl, but he had a hard time showing it. He was looking for a better place than his parents' farm in Arkansas, which he had inherited upon their death. He had recently sold the farm and planned on settling out west.

After settling the matter, Bob went to tend to Esther, and Elizabeth noticed that Bill had caught the eye of a pretty, redheaded girl, who was traveling with a family from Mississippi. Bill didn't walk right up and start talking to her, but Elizabeth could tell he was interested. So, she made a point of starting a conversation with her.

"Did I hear you say your family is from Mississippi?"

"Yes, and where are you and your brother from?"

"We're from Davenport, Iowa, ma'am," Bill replied, in a barely audible mumble.

"I'm Elizabeth Dedmore, and this is my brother, Bill."

"Pleased to meet you. I'm Susan Smith," the girl said with a not-so-shy look toward Bill. "Why are you traveling to California?" Susan continued, trying to draw Bill out.

"I'm going to strike it rich in the goldfields." Bill spoke a little louder and met Susan's gaze. "And my sister is going to join her fiancé, who's already there in Grass Valley, California. Why are you going?"

"My dad wants to strike it rich, too, so it looks like we're going all the way to Northern California together," she said with anticipation in her voice.

"Yes, ma'am," Bill replied, as he appraised the redhead with an admiring gaze.

Elizabeth wandered to the opposite side of the campfire to resume talking to Bob Sterling, but she kept an eye on her brother talking to the pretty redhead and tried to see her brother through the eyes of this engaging, young lady, Susan. She probably saw Bill as a little shy but very handsome and adventurous to want to go all the way to California to make his fortune. She imagined Susan thought he was definitely someone she'd like to get to know better.

Susan turned to another young lady she had just met. "Betsy, what do you look forward to on this adventure we are starting?"

"I've heard so much about all the handsome cowboys out west, I am dying to meet one or maybe two."

Susan laughed, and her reply was lost in the hubbub of the pioneers milling about the campfire.

The White family was also at that campfire that night. Bill and Elizabeth heard the mother say to her son, "Steward, do you see that pretty, redheaded girl over there? She would make a good match for you."

Steward, who was not shy at all and very independent, had already noticed Susan and had designs on her, but he said to his mother, "I'm of age, Mother. I'll choose who I do or don't pursue."

"Well, since you've decided to come west with us after all, the least you can do is accept our help finding a decent match for you," his mother reprimanded her son.

"Oh, Isabel, leave the boy alone," his father said wearily. Elizabeth raised her eyebrows at Bill as if to say, *This family is going to be trouble.*

Later that night, as they rolled out their beds preparing for sleep, she warned her brother, "If you like that girl Susan, you are going to have some competition from that guy Steward."

Bill said nothing, but his smirk said that he wasn't worried about a little competition.

Elizabeth sighed. Her brother certainly had a long way to go in learning some humility, but she guessed that was something that he would have to learn naturally.

Early the next morning, Elizabeth and Bill met the wagon scout, Joseph Walker. He was going from wagon to wagon introducing himself to the pioneers. Several children, mostly boys, followed him with admiration. He was an imposing figure, standing six feet, four inches tall and weighing two hundred pounds—a real mountain man.

Bill lost some of his shyness around Walker. "How old are you now, Mr. Walker?" he asked.

"Well, I don't mind telling you, I'm fifty-five. I've been around a lot, and I've got tales to tell you that would astound you."

Walker was a self-confident leader among the Western men as well as the Eastern folks who had committed to become Westerners. He wore leather britches with a matching jacket and a coonskin cap that only added to his appeal as a seasoned mountain man.

"I sure want to hear those tales," Elizabeth added, very impressed by her first meeting with the legendary trapper, explorer, and scout.

He didn't stay long but moved on to the next wagon and offered to help an inexperienced tenderfoot hook up their team of horses to their wagon.

Bill, too, was impressed with someone who seemed destined to live up to his legend and could mentor him and steer him on the right paths in life.

That morning, the site of the wagon train gathering for departure was barely organized chaos. There was dust being thrown up by the horses, mules, and oxen being hitched up to the wagons. There were cries of the pioneers calling goodbyes to those left behind. There was excitement in the air from the anticipation and some trepidation for the adventure about to get underway.

Many of the pioneers gathered were inexperienced city folk and had to be instructed on the ways of wagon train travel. The more experienced members of the train assisted Riker and Walker in their endeavors to get the train ready to depart.

Bill was showing Elizabeth how to hitch up their team of oxen, a skill she had not needed to know until now.

"What did you do with the spare oxen?" she asked.

"They are in with the remuda," replied Bill. "I had to mark them, so we can identify them as ours."

Bob Sterling, although very busy getting his own family and their wagon ready for the start of the journey, found time to come by Bill and Elizabeth's wagon and ask if they needed any help.

Bill smirked at his sister and replied for them, "Thanks, Mr. Sterling, but we have everything under control."

Several hours later, after Riker, Walker, and their helpers had made inspections of every wagon and team, and they were satisfied all was properly prepared, Captain Riker gave the command, "Wagons, ho!"

Bill whipped up his team of oxen and said with excitement in his voice, "Finally, we're headed west. I'm sure going to enjoy this trip. How about you, Sis?"

There was no response from Elizabeth as she gritted her teeth and held on tight.

Chapter Five

THE SEARCH FOR THE SWEDE'S GOLD

GRASS VALLEY GOLDFIELD, CALIFORNIA

JUNE 25, 1853

A few days later, Greta tried to get her brother Sven to play with two little stray kittens that they had found. It was Long John's turn to care for the children. They were in his front yard under a spreading oak tree. Sven still hadn't said a word since the accident that killed his pappy.

"Can we keep them, Long John?" implored Greta. One kitten had crawled onto Greta's lap, and the other one was on Sven's lap. They were sitting on an old log that had fallen in a bad storm last winter. Both kittens were purring in contentment as the children petted them. Sven's kitten had a normal purr, but Greta's had a loud, rough-sounding purr that was very distinct.

"Now, Kids," Long John responded, "I don't know. I don't have time to care for two stray cats as well as two children. It's up to Jason, I reckon; he'll be your pappy as soon as he gets well enough."

"I'm naming mine Sally. She looks like a Sally." Sally had jumped down and was busy playing with Greta's tattered dress, a strip of which hung down almost to the ground. Greta stood up and took a step away, but the calico kitten hung on tight and was being dragged along. Sven's kitten was gray with only a little bit of tabby mixed in.

Not to be outdone by his sister, Sven replied, "I'm naming mine Star. See the star on his forehead?"

"You're talking again!" Greta exclaimed and ran over to hug her brother in her excitement.

"Yours is a silly Sally. Look at how silly she is."

"I like that, Sven. Her name is Silly Sally."

"How do you know it's a she?"

"How do you know yours is a he?" Greta asked. How can we tell, Long John?" She looked over at him.

Long John replied, "It's hard to tell, but if you have two kittens to compare, it's easier. Lift up their tails."

Greta picked up her kitten again, and each child lifted up their kittens' tails.

Long John continued, "If the distance between those two dots is bigger, it's a boy. If it's closer, it's a girl."

"Mine is bigger than yours; see, Star is a boy," Sven exclaimed.

"Yes, and mine's a girl, just like I said."

Long John cautioned the kids, "Now don't you two get too attached to those kittens, just in case Jason says no to you keeping them." But the children continued to play with their new pets, as Long John worked on repairing some of his mining equipment.

Jason was starting to feel somewhat better. He swept up another pile of debris in the Sphensons' house, one-handed, using a broom with a short handle. He was still somewhat awkward with only a left hand. He could handle the clean-up with the broom, but he would have to ask for help in repairing the furniture.

The kids were playing with their new kittens in their front yard. Jason didn't have the heart to deny them the pleasure of keeping the kittens after losing their pappy.

The Sphensons' house—though only a shanty, barely twelve feet by twenty feet—was certainly better than the makeshift lean-to he had constructed for himself. His next job, after sweeping up, was to repair the cots and table that had been damaged, he assumed, when the place had been torn apart while the vandals were looking for Sphenson's gold stash. He had a good idea who the vandals were—Luke and Stephen.

The two greedy miners were seen leaving the Sphenson house by Long John when he took over watching the children. They were the ones most curious about what happened to the Swede's missing gold. Luke and Stephen were reportedly still trying to recruit for McKnight, so Jason surmised that they probably hadn't found anything.

Sven sat quietly in the dirt of the front yard with his kitten Star asleep in his lap. The boy still didn't talk much, ever since the death of his pappy. His older sister Greta sat beside him, watching her kitten chasing dust mites that were dancing in the sunbeams from the late afternoon sunlight slanting through the pine boughs.

"Look at that, Silly Sally. Who else would be happy chasing sunbeams?" Greta asked. She bent down and scooped up Silly Sally and plopped the calico into her lap. The kitten immediately began her rusty-sounding purr, content with her new mistress.

Jason picked up one of the broken chairs and stood in the doorway and watched the children and their kittens for some time. Finally, he said to the kids, "Put the kittens away in their box. We have to go to the general store."

As Jason approached the general store, he recalled being told that the long, sturdy, log structure had been one of the first built along Wolf Creek back in '49. The store occupied about half of it, and Roussiere lived in the other half. Jason found a couple of the miners hanging around the front boardwalk and enlisted their help in repairing the busted-up furniture in the kids' house.

Roussiere himself came out just as they were leaving. He said, "Jason, I've been meaning to talk to you. I'm in need of help with my store. Would you be interested in taking a clerk's job?"

Jason was momentarily taken aback. He thought a minute and then said, "I had not considered doing anything like that. Are you sure? I'm missing one arm. Are you sure it won't get in the way of me doing my job?"

Roussiere replied, "I've given it some thought, and I think you'll do just fine. I still have a strong back for any heavy lifting, and you know how to do your sums good enough to take payments. You've had some college training as I understand it, right?"

Jason nodded in agreement. "Yes, sir. I've had two years of engineering. Will it be okay if I take some time to give it some serious thought and get back to you?"

"Sure, take all the time you need. You know where to find me."

Jason was trying to see if he could still pan for gold like he used to before his accident. He stood knee-deep in Wolf Creek and held his gold pan in his left hand. He scooped up sand and gravel from the stream. He swished it around and let the light stuff spill over and back into the stream. He closely examined what remained in the pan and saw some likely gold specks. He jammed the pan under the stump of his right arm and held it rather precariously while he picked out the gold particles from the pan. He headed to the stream bank to set his pan down but stumbled on a loose rock and dropped the pan—and the gold particles, as well—back into the creek.

"This will never work! I guess I'd better take Roussiere up on his offer."

When he gave Roussiere his decision, Jason said, "My only concern is who will take care of the children while I'm at work."

"I'll only need you about twenty hours a week to start with. How about if you bring the kids with you when you come? We'll find something to keep them occupied. They'll be in school, once the summer's over anyhow."

###

Stephen was questioning the Sphenson kids the next day in their front yard, while Luke looked on. It was morning, and Stephen had babysitting duty. The children were playing with their stick horses.

"So, you kids don't have any idea where your old pappy might have hidden something valuable?"

"What kind of valuables you talking about?" Greta asked.

"Oh, ya know, something like his or your ma's wedding ring or a locket he might've given your ma." Stephen threw Luke a quick glance; they had agreed not to reveal they were looking for the gold stash.

"Ma never had no locket, and I think she still wore her wedding ring when we buried her," Greta replied.

Stephen looked at Luke in exasperation.

Luke tried his luck. "Where did your pappy keep the stuff he had in his pockets when he went to sleep at night?"

Greta replied, "He put that stuff under his pillow; but someone tore up our house, and we couldn't even find the pillow or much else either."

Stephen jumped back in again. "Now, see here, little girl, we're trying to help you kids out. You're without a ma and pa, and you'll need help getting by. We're here to help you, so you got to help us."

Sven broke down, and his sky-blue eyes started leaking tears. Greta tried to comfort him while shooting Stephen a reproachful look for using that tone of voice and bringing up their late parents. With her arms around her little brother hugging him tight, Greta turned her back on the men, protecting them from the cruel world, her long, blonde hair spilling over Sven's hair, of the same color, as if to aid in protecting him.

Later that night, Luke and Stephen were at the campfire with the group of independent miners, trying once again to recruit someone.

"I just spent ten hours standing in freezing water working my claim by hand with nothing to show for it," Long John complained.

"I know what you mean," another miner named Mike responded. "Most of the loose gold in the streams around Boston Ravine is panned out."

"Haven't you heard? They're calling it Grass Valley nowadays," Luke remarked.

"I thought it was renamed Centerville," chimed in another miner.

Stephen cut in, "Maybe we should reconsider going to work for one of the quartz mines. I heard McKnight's hiring over at Gold Hill."

"You won't catch me in one of those dark, dirty mine shafts. I'd feel like the walls were closing in, and it'd be hard to breathe," Long John replied.

"Maybe so, but at least you got something to show for your day's work. It sure beats slaving all day for nothing."

"I hear they had another cave-in at North Star this week," said Mike.

"I don't trust those La Vance Brothers and all those other Frenchmen at the Helvetia and Lafayette Gold Mining Company," Pete remarked. "They are so tight-fisted; their tunnels aren't safe."

Luke muttered low, so only Stephen could hear, "We're running out of time; we need to convince someone to work for McKnight."

As the group broke up for the night, the two disgruntled recruiters complained as they made their way back to their cabin.

"This trying to get placer miners to turn around and become hard rock miners isn't working," Luke said.

"We need to concentrate on finding the late Swede's stash. That's a surer deal," Stephen insisted.

Luke nodded in agreement as they forded Wolf Creek to get to their cabin.

It was Jason's first day working at Roussiere's General Store. He was dressed in clean clothes, had trimmed his beard, and had on his new wooden arm that Adam had carved for him.

When Adam had come with Marcos to fit it to Jason's arm, he had been embarrassed at first to expose his crippled arm; but when Marcos secured the bindings and Jason rolled down his long sleeve shirt, Jason commented, "It almost looks normal. You did a good job, Adam. Thank you very much."

"Those who don't have real money pay in gold dust," Roussiere was now instructing Jason. "Here, I'll show you how to weigh the gold on my scale and convert it to dollars and cents." He showed Jason his scale and how to use it. He opened the safe where the accumulated gold was stored, careful to keep the combination to himself. "When we get enough gold, I will take it to either the Wells Fargo office in Nevada City or to the mint in San Francisco. We get a slightly better exchange rate at the mint, but I don't get to San Francisco that often."

Jason soon learned it was common practice for store owners to take gold as payment for goods at two dollars per ounce under what they could get for it at the mint in San Francisco.

He noticed Roussiere watching rather closely when Jason waited on customers, but he understood. He was judging Jason's honesty with money, which was only natural. After a few hours, Roussiere seemed satisfied and found other things to do.

The children were trying to entertain themselves without much luck while Jason worked.

"Papa Jason, I'm bored. What can Sven and I do?" Greta complained.

Roussiere overheard this and came forward. "Here is an old children's book, left here by a miner who left last year."

Jason glanced through the book, titled *Der Struwwelpeter.* "Is this in German or French?" he asked.

"I think it's German, but does it matter? I doubt if the children can read, anyway. They can look at the pictures."

Greta was happy with the book, showing Sven the pictures and trying to sound out the funny writing that went along with each picture.

Jason asked Roussiere, "Do you know any Germans in the goldfield?"

"There's George D. Roberts; I understand he speaks German."

"I'll contact him and see if he would tell me more about this book and maybe translate it," Jason said.

Jason swept off the porch of the general store. He stopped a moment to look out across the lush, green expanse of Grass Valley. Roussiere built his cabin on a ravine near Wolf Creek with a good view of the growing township. Jason saw horses and buggies, miners on foot, and carpenters at work building various structures.

Most of the trees that dotted the valley had been cleared to make room for the buildings. They had provided the wood to build the houses and businesses of the new settlement.

Jason heard the pounding of hammers and the rhythmic swish of handsaws cutting the lumber. He saw draft horses harnessed and pulling out stumps to clear sites for buildings that would soon be up. He also saw Chinese laborers helping with the construction because this was one of the few tasks they were allowed to do in gold camps. There were natives, too, doing odd jobs around the gold camp.

"Say, Jason," commented Roussiere, "did you know when California became a U. S. Territory in 1847, the natives were informed that they had to obey the laws made by the white men's government? Some of the laws were quite harsh. For instance, any native caught stealing a horse was to be shot. If a native was caught killing or stealing cattle, they were to be flogged. Natives could charge a white man with wrongdoing, but this had to be tried and settled in a white man's court. No white man could be convicted of any crime on merely the testimony of a native. Any native employed by a white man had to carry papers or a certificate of employment. Most natives did not understand the value of gold."

"I might hire a native or a Chinese to work for me," replied Jason, "since I can't work my placer claim anymore. I think I'll try to find one who knows the value of gold, although it might be helpful if they didn't to curtail thefts."

"I'm glad to see you aren't prejudiced against the natives or the Chinese, Jason. In our business, we must serve the customer, no matter the color of their skin."

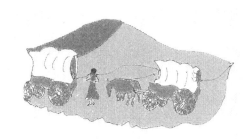

Chapter Six

THE RIVALRY BEGINS

SOMEWHERE IN MISSOURI

JULY 1, 1853

One day, Walker, who was returning from scouting, spotted a small herd of buffalo. He rode into camp just as the wagons were circling up for the night. "Who wants to shoot your dinner tonight? There's buffalo just over that rise."

Bill was the first one to grab his rifle and join Walker, who led a small group of men and some boys up a sagebrush-covered rise to the top of a slight hill, where they could see the buffalo grazing.

Elizabeth and a few of the women who were curious about the buffalo followed behind the men.

Walker instructed the group of mostly inexperienced hunters on how to sneak up on the herd down-wind, so they would not alert them with their human scent.

They found a convenient grove of trees within fifty yards of some stragglers in the herd, and they all found boulders and trees for cover.

"Now, everyone, take careful aim because after the first shot, that herd will likely spook and stampede away."

Steward was lined up next to Bill. On Walker's command, a volley of shots rang out. True to his prediction, it sent the herd stampeding away. There was only one buffalo that dropped from all the shots. Bill was not shy in saying that it was the buffalo he'd aimed at.

Steward said loud so everyone could hear, "I was aiming at that buffalo, too; it could have been my shot that brought it down."

Walker replied, "Not likely since you're shooting a shot gun not a rifle."

While Bill was basking in the admiration of the other youths, Elizabeth and the women set upon the downed carcass to cut out their dinner. Elizabeth stood there scratching her head, wondering which part to start with. Mabel, an older, more experienced lady married to a butcher, jumped right in and sliced off part of the hump and started on her way back to camp. After the other ladies sliced off stakes for their families, it barely made a dent in the immense animal.

Elizabeth lamented the waste of the rest of the buffalo but said, "What can we do? There is no way to keep the meat preserved unless we take the time to smoke it. We should advise the rest of the pioneers about getting their share of readily available buffalo." She hesitated a moment, then went back and sliced off some more to cook and take for later.

The next morning, Elizabeth struggled with the normal breakfast meal on the trail Bill came by while she was scratching her head and tugging her ear.

"What's for breakfast, Sis?"

"We're having bacon and bread," she replied as she placed the iron skillet over the coals of the cooking fire. She unwrapped the bacon and sliced off thick pieces to add to the pan when it got hot enough. "There are a few beans left over from supper last night," she added.

"This is the last of the bread," Bill remarked.

"That means I'll have to take the time to bake some more. Can you get out the Dutch oven for me?"

"Is the coffee ready?"

"Yes, but mind that it's hot."

While Elizabeth prepared the bread, she filled Bill in on meals for the rest of the day. "The noon meal will have to be coffee, beans, and bacon or more of that extra buffalo I went back for. The evening meals will be boiled rice with buffalo, if there is any left."

The Riker wagon train stopped near Independence, Missouri. It was July fourth. Everyone wanted to take the time to observe Independence Day.

The men went hunting and happened upon a flock of wild turkeys. This provided something special to feast on. Bill showed off his growing skill with his rifle by hitting and killing a big tom gobbler. Some of the men, including Steward, hunted with shotguns. He managed on his third try to down a turkey as well. When he brought it to his mother to clean and cook, she took one look at the mangled bird and said, "You shot it, you clean it; and be sure to get all those buck shots out."

For the Fourth of July celebration, Susan and her mother decided to make molasses pudding for dessert for her family and Elizabeth and Bill, as well. Susan took the opportunity to give Elizabeth a cooking lesson. She had some fresh milk. She was one of the pioneers who'd brought along cows for milk. They were also able to make butter from the milk. They would often milk their cows first thing in the morning before starting off on their journey. They simply stored the fresh milk in a covered bucket tied onto their wagon. If the weather wasn't too hot, by the time they camped for the night, the jostling of the wagon had turned the milk into butter.

Susan instructed Elizabeth on how to blend the molasses and milk. "Now, add in the butter, baking soda, and salt; and mix it all well."

"This butter isn't mixing well," complained Elizabeth.

"The butter will remain chunky," Susan noted. "Now, add in the flour, half a cup at a time. Next comes the raisins. Now, you pour this thick dough into a deep bread pan that I've buttered, spreading it evenly. Here comes the tricky part. Put the pan in a large kettle of slow-boiling, shallow water."

"Like this?" Elizabeth asked, as she set the pan directly over the fire.

"No, it has to sit on the pebbles at the edge in a low fire."

"Make sure the liquid only goes about halfway up the sides of the pan," Susan's mother cautioned.

"How long will it take to cook?" Elizabeth asked.

"It has to steam for one-and-a-quarter hours," Susan replied.

When done, they served the pudding in slices. The boiled pudding had the texture of cake. It was topped with maple syrup.

"That was delicious pudding. Good job," Susan's mother complimented the cooks.

After eating their fill of the welcome addition of roast turkey and the rare treat of molasses pudding for dessert, Elizabeth, Susan, and Bill joined the other pioneers who were assembling a makeshift band. The band didn't have a leader but included a fiddle, a mouth harp, a banjo, and several guitars. The pioneers danced around the campfire, and someone produced a copy of the Declaration of Independence, which was read to the group.

Bill hung around with Steward.

"Are you going to ask anyone to dance?" Steward asked Bill. Neither of the youths had gotten up enough nerve to ask one of the girls to dance.

Bill wanted to ask Susan to dance but hadn't got up the nerve yet.

Steward finally said, "Well, if you aren't going to ask Susan to dance, I will."

Bill reacted, a stab of jealousy spearing his heart as Susan accepted Steward's invitation and he led her to the end of the square dance line. Bill started toward them, but then stopped. *I'll get my chance*, he thought to himself.

But as he watched them dance, Bill fumed inwardly, *You're pushing it, Boy. Wait until I get my hands on you. Hey, you're holding her way too tight! I'll show you; just give me a chance.*

His chance finally came when the dancing was almost over. Steward returned from the dance area. The band started playing a waltz. Bill saw that it was now or never with Susan. He steeled up his nerve, walked over, and asked, "Can I have this dance?"

"I thought you'd never ask," she replied as Bill took her into his arms. The top of Susan's head came just to Bill's chin. Susan laid her cheek on Bill's chest. *Wow! She fits perfectly in my arms.*

They floated around the campfire, and everyone else seemed to disappear to the young couple. The revelry lasted until around midnight. After the crowd broke up, Susan allowed Bill to take her hand as he walked her back to her wagon.

The Riker Wagon Train arrived at Fort Dodge on the south bank of the Arkansas River late on the evening of July 30, 1853. They'd been traveling for only forty days across Missouri and the Kansas Territory, but Elizabeth complained to Bill that it seemed like forty weeks.

The wagon train waited on the banks of the river to discuss how the crossing would best be accomplished. Riker told the assembled pioneers, "There's a ferry that'll take your wagons across for a fee, but you'll have to wait in line. I advise those of you who didn't waterproof your wagons to take the ferry."

Some of those without waterproofing were too impatient to wait for the ferry. One of these asked, "Why can't we rely on the scout, Walker, to point out the shallowest place to cross on our own?"

Walker replied, "I'd advise against that. The water's just too deep."

But some thought by watching where others crossed safely and following right behind, they could make it okay. Unfortunately, some of them didn't.

Walker tried his best to help these unfortunates, but he could only do so much. One wagon filled up so fast, it literally sank, and Walker had to cut loose the team and leave the wagon and all its goods behind.

Walker told Bill and Elizabeth, "Most travelers remain on the north side of the Arkansas River until at least Bent's Fort, but I find this crossing better than the one later. Believe me, that one is even deeper with the amount of water flowing just now."

Bob Sterling had insisted on crossing with his own wagon and then returning and crossing with Elizabeth's wagon. Elizabeth had shown appreciation for the favor, but Bill had the feeling Bob was inserting himself into her affairs for ulterior motives. Elizabeth had confided in him that she was afraid those motives had to do with acquiring a new mother for his little girl.

Bill kept an eye on Susan and her family's wagon as it crossed the river. He reined up his horse to let the wagon catch up to him, and suddenly, he saw a large tree floating in the current, heading right toward Susan's wagon. He yelled a warning, but the noise of the wagons crossing the river drowned out his shout.

He reached for his lasso and guided his horse within range. He was thankful for Walker's lessons on handling a lasso. He lassoed one of the branches and pulled his mount around to redirect the tree away from Susan's wagon. He only partially succeeded in his efforts. A submerged branch from the tree caught on a wagon wheel and jerked the wagon, and Susan, riding on the passenger side, catapulted into the river.

Bill dropped his rope, rather than taking the time to unhook it from the tree, and headed toward the floundering girl. When he got to her, he reached down and pulled her up with him onto the horse. She was dripping wet, but when she realized who rescued her, she threw her arms around Bill and hugged him tight.

Later, after all the wagons had made the crossing, Bill rode up to Elizabeth as she stood by their wagon with Bob and said, "You made it okay, Lizzy. I was keeping my eye on you as best I could."

"Oh, yeah? It looked to me like you were keeping both eyes—and at least one of your hands—on Susan." Elizabeth laughed when she said it, though.

Elizabeth had nothing against Susan and Bill as a couple. In fact, she thought Susan would be quite a catch for Bill. She seemed very outgoing and friendly to everyone and might seem like a flirt to some people, being young and full of life. But Elizabeth knew from her interaction with the family that her mother and father had instilled in her good, moral values and an honest work ethic. She knew that Susan cooked most of the meals for her family as well as having chores like feeding the animals and collecting firewood or buffalo chips for the nightly campfires. She was, in fact, teaching Elizabeth how to cook.

"Yes, Bill, we made it, thanks to Mr. Sterling. I'm sure glad we had the blacksmith in St. Louis caulk our wagon, so it would keep our goods dry during river crossings."

Elizabeth turned to Mr. Sterling with a smile. "Thank you, Mr. Sterling, for helping with our wagon and for loaning me a horse to cross on myself. You will have to show me how to drive a wagon across a river by myself—on a smaller river, of course."

"We'll see about that. Now I have to go see about my own wagon." Mr. Sterling turned its care back over to a fifteen-year-old boy he'd hired for most of his own driving. It was worth the expense to impress Elizabeth. He was glad he'd successfully crossed the major obstacle of the Arkansas River safely himself.

But Elizabeth wasn't a fool. She suspected his intent in helping her was to make her more dependent on him and his assistance.

Elizabeth was glad, in a way, that she had a chance to take a bath while crossing the river. Even on horseback, she found she and her clothes were soaked. The dust and grime from walking all day in the hot July sun took its toll. She was looking forward to a break at Fort Dodge before heading off into the New Mexico Territory on the Santa Fe Trail.

The Riker Wagon Train formed up in the traditional circle just outside the Fort Dodge stockade. They did this, not so much to protect against hostile natives this time but to form containment for the livestock. Bill was happy about this decision because it meant he didn't have to worry about night herding duty, a job he often got stuck doing.

"Lizzy, are you coming with us to see Fort Dodge?" Quite a town had grown up around the frontier fort.

"It's tempting. I'd love to get a real meal that I don't have to make myself. But I'm so tired, I think I'll just collapse and go to sleep right after supper." Elizabeth slipped into the wagon and accessed her secret hiding place and got enough money for Bill to pay for his supper. "Now, you stay out of trouble, you hear me!"

"Ah, Sis, you know me better than that."

But she saw him leave with Steward, who had managed to get them into trouble more than once. She shook her head in exasperation. *I trust you but not that guy you're with.*

After supper, she said goodnight to the few wagon train members who had not gone into town and retired to her wagon. For the first time, there was more than enough room for her to stretch out, and she took advantage of the luxury. *I'll not have this much room once we stock up on supplies before we continue.* Then slumber overtook her.

###

The two boys strode down the main street in Fort Dodge. Every other business was a saloon or a bordello, it seemed.

"Hey, Bill," said Steward, "let's check out Stoky's Saloon."

"Na, we haven't seen half the town yet," Bill replied.

Steward went along, for now. He knew there would be other chances to get a drink and have some fun.

A little later, as they came out of the livery stable, they saw a native in a buckskin robe sitting in front of a store.

"Watch this," Steward said. He detoured up on the boardwalk, and striding by the unsuspecting native, he grabbed a feather from his headband. The man, who was too drunk to react, just sat there.

"That's not nice, Steward," Bill scolded him.

"It's just an old, drunken native." Further down the street, Steward said, "Let's see what's going on down that alley."

Just then they saw familiar figures come stumbling out of the alley. It was Joseph Walker, and he was supporting none other than Bob Sterling.

Bill was too shocked to say or do anything. He just stepped aside as the duo stumbled past them.

The next morning, Elizabeth rose early as usual and ran into Joseph Walker.

"Morning, Miss Dedmore," he greeted her. "How did you survive that river crossing yesterday?"

"Good morning, Joseph. We all survived just fine, thanks to Bob Sterling. He insisted on driving my wagon across."

"Ma'am, I hear you're betrothed to a miner out in the California goldfields. I'd be careful of that Bob Sterling; he's not to be trusted."

"Why do you say that? He's been nothing but a gentleman to me and a tremendous help on our journey."

"Ma'am, I don't see him as a boy, a rowdy young man, or a ruffian. But he is a reveler. I've been around a lot, and I have a sixth sense about smelling out a deadbeat. Believe me, he doesn't want to see you safely reach them goldfields and reunite with your fellow."

"I don't know what to think."

Joseph Walker just gave Elizabeth a knowing look and went on his way.

Elizabeth puzzled on this warning all morning. Could there be more to Bob Sterling's solicitous behavior than meets the eye?

Later that afternoon, Elizabeth drove her wagon into Fort Dodge to stock up on trail supplies. Bill accompanied her to help with the lifting and packing.

"Billy, Joseph Walker said something to me this morning about not trusting Bob Sterling. You've had more chances to observe Bob and what he says around other people. What do you know about that?"

Bill hesitated, then said, "He is sweet on you, and anyone could see that. He needs someone to take care of his little girl, and you certainly have become friends with her. And I asked you to call me Bill from now on."

"Sorry, I forgot. I've grown to love his daughter, and I hope I've done Esther some good, but any gentleman would respect that I'm engaged. So, you haven't heard or seen him say or do anything that would make you think he was unscrupulous?"

Bill thought back to the evening before when he saw Bob and Joseph coming out of the back entrance of the saloon in Fort Dodge. He hadn't had a chance to talk to Joseph about the incident yet. He planned on telling her about Bob, but he didn't want to besmirch the name of his hero, Joseph Walker. So, he decided not to say anything to Elizabeth until he checked with Walker.

"Not really, but then I'm not around him that much. I will pay more attention to him from now on and let you know if I do."

"I would appreciate that. You're a good brother, but you're a poor chaperone."

Bill had spent more time enjoying his favorite passions, camping and exploring. He'd become good friends with Walker, often accompanying him on his scouting trips for the wagon train. It had allowed Elizabeth more room and privacy at nighttime with Bill sleeping outdoors under the stars, so she hadn't complained.

###

Bill was finishing packing the wagon with the goods they'd purchased in Fort Dodge, but when Elizabeth came out with the last load of their purchases, he was standing by their wagon scratching his head. "What's the problem, little brother?" she asked.

"We've got too much stuff; it doesn't all fit in our wagon."

Elizabeth looked and had to laugh at the mess Bill had made of packing the supplies. "Let me see what I can do with this," she said. Her analytical, organized mind saw the problem. She instructed Bill to take out the heavy boxes, so they could be placed on the bottom. She had Bill balance them out to distribute the load evenly. Then they placed the lighter items around the edges of the wagon to leave room in case someone had to ride inside.

While his sister was rearranging their supplies, Susan and her family came out of the store, and she stopped to talk to Bill. "Did you get everything you need?" she asked.

"Yes, and then some," Bill replied.

"This is the last big outpost before we get to Santa Fe. We should make sure we have everything we will possibly need," Susan said.

"I think we're well stocked. Have you had a chance to see much of Fort Dodge?"

"Not really," Susan replied. "I was thinking of walking back to the wagon train—if I had someone to accompany me."

"There. That should do it." Elizabeth clambered from the back of their wagon onto the seat. She had overheard Susan's remark and said, "Go ahead, Bill, and walk the lady back. I'll be fine."

Bill had already seen a good deal of the growing town the evening before, so when Susan took his arm, he purposely took a different route back to the train. Their walk took them past the sheriff's office and jail, and Susan exclaimed, "Look, the sheriff is arresting someone."

Bill detoured them to the other side of the street, and they stopped to watch a tough-looking lawman prodding a dejected cowboy toward the jail. "That must be the newly elected sheriff, James Doty. He is taking over law enforcement because the army is pulling out of Fort Dodge later this year."

"You're so smart, Bill. How do you know all that stuff?"

Actually, Elizabeth had found out from a talkative store clerk and filled Bill in earlier. But Bill didn't mind looking good in Susan's eyes, so he just nodded and said, "People talk if you're listening."

After a day's layover for the members to resupply, the wagon train set out again. Joseph Walker led them west on the Santa Fe Trail.

Bill rode with Walker, who expounded on the various native tribes. They were traveling up a ridge that led to a plateau where they could get a good view of the terrain ahead. Bill loved hearing tales of wilderness adventure from the old mountain man. But the incident yesterday in the alley in Fort Dodge bothered him. He mulled over the possibilities in his mind for a while. Finally, he couldn't stand it anymore, and he blurted out, "What were you doing in that alley behind the Watering Hole Saloon with Bob Sterling yesterday?"

"What? I thought it was obvious. I was trying to get Bob Sterling back to the wagon train in one piece."

"So, you weren't drunk or visiting the ladies who work in the saloon?"

"Do I look hung over? Besides, I have a wife waiting for me in California."

Bill thought about it a while. Finally, he decided to trust the scout. "I believe you. But what was Bob Sterling doing there?"

"I was just walking by the place on my way back from getting a haircut when Bob came staggering out. I thought the least I could do was make sure he got back to the wagon train okay. I did warn your sister about putting too much trust in that Sterling fellow."

Bill was satisfied. He greatly appreciated Walker's wealth of information and sage advice. "Now, what were you saying?"

"We'll be traveling through the land designated for the Choctaw nation. The Choctaw, for the most part, are friendly to wagon trains just passing through, but there are always those renegades who still resent being relocated from their native lands in the East and South. I wasn't part of that relocation, so I get along okay with the Choctaw."

Walker continued, "Personally I think the Choctaw got a raw deal. President Jackson signed the Indian Removal Act some twenty years ago. Thousands of Choctaws were forced from their native-held land in the cotton kingdom east of the Mississippi. They were moved to reservations on lands to the west in the native colonization zone that the United States had acquired as part of the Louisiana Purchase. In 1831, the Choctaw tribe was the first to be relocated."

"Did they get horses to ride?"

"No, they made the journey on foot. Some were bound in chains and marched double file."

"On foot? How far are you talking about?" Bill asked incredulously.

"Some had to travel over a thousand miles. They were without any food, supplies, or other help from the government. Thousands of people died along the way. I read in an Alabama newspaper it was a trail of tears and death."

"That doesn't seem right," Bill lamented.

They traveled in silent commiseration, thinking about the Choctaws' desperate plight.

With a heavy sigh, Bill changed the subject. "Did you help survey this trail we will be taking for the mail express route?"

"Yes, I did, last year. This route was chosen for its easier terrain and fewer river crossings and because it goes through safer territory. Riker wanted to use the Santa Fe Trail to start our journey because he's most familiar with it. From Santa Fe on, we'll follow the Southern Overland Trail route. As I was helping lay out that trail, it occurred to me it's a far better wagon train trail to California than the ones further north we'd used before. It's especially good for those trains that got a late start, like Riker's, because it's farther south so we don't have to worry about snow and mountains in September and October."

"Is this the first wagon train you have guided on this trail?" Bill asked.

"Yes, and I think it'll probably be the last. There's a beautiful piece of land in Contra Costa on the California coast I've got my eye on. I plan on settling down there when I give up scouting for wagon trains."

"You've told me about your adventures leading parties west. What about any adventures heading east?"

"Why, yes, I recollect one time back in 1834, I was leading a party east, and we got stuck in the Nevada desert. It got so bad, we had to drink the blood of our horses that had died in order to survive. Then we got attacked by natives. Even though we killed fourteen of them without a loss of any of our men, it was touch-and-go until we made it to the Bear River."

They had attained the plateau and sat their mounts to survey the hills and gullies of the land they were heading into.

"What is California like?"

"Well, when I was there last, I saw giant sequoia and redwood trees that reach almost to Heaven. But there are also earthquakes that shake the ground like you wouldn't believe. You can't imagine what it's like to see the Pacific Ocean for the first time. Have you ever seen an ocean?"

"No, and I'm really looking forward to it."

"Then, we'd better keep moving."

As Bill and Walker scouted ahead of the wagon train, Walker taught Bill how to improve his tracking skills. He sat high in a juniper tree waiting for his young student to decipher and follow his tracks. He'd instructed Bill to give him a half-hour head start, and that was over an hour ago.

Joseph was a man who enjoyed the solitude of the wilderness. This place where he now sat reminded him of what was important in life. Nature spoke to him better than any man could. *The wind pushing through the leaves of the juniper trees seem to blow away the cares that weigh down my mind.* Sometimes the responsibility of leading so many people across the mountains got to him. *I just need to take a little time to calm my mind. I need to slow down the pace, and a place like this is just what I need.*

He heard a rustling in the sagebrush, and Bill appeared with his head down, studying the ground before him. Joseph smiled in pleasure. He'd not left an easy trail to follow. He was proud of Bill, but he let him stop at the juniper tree to pounder which way the trail went from there. After giving him several minutes, Joseph finally took mercy on the puzzled lad and spoke up. "Good job, Bill."

Bill jumped a foot into the air. "You scared the devil out of me."

"Always be aware of your surroundings. Look up as well as down. Danger may come from the least likely direction."

"Did you ever get surprised from an unexpected attack?" Bill asked, as they led their horses down a steep bluff.

"I did. I recollect back in 1833 when Captain Benjamin Bonneville suggested I take my first party to California. I left the Green River, where we had been trapping beaver, with a party of forty men in August. Bonneville claimed we could get a much better price for our furs in Los Angeles. Each man took four horses, one to ride and three to carry supplies. The supplies included sixty pounds of dried meat per man. When we reached Salt Lake, we met up with some Bannock natives. We asked them what the best route west would be. We decided to follow their advice and took the Humboldt River into the area called Nevada. We made good progress for a while, but in September, we were surprised by around eight hundred natives in the area that was called Alta California then."

"Wow, that's a lot of natives. What was Alta California? I've never heard of that part of California," said Bill.

"That is what they used to call Northern California when it first became a territory. Because of the California Gold Rush that used emigrant trails through the area, Alta California became part of the Utah Territory.

"Getting back to my story, the natives surrounded our party and attacked us. We were forced to fight back. It turned out they had never seen guns before, so after we had killed thirty-nine of them, they decided to retreat.

"Soon afterwards, we reached the Sierra Nevada Mountains. The climb was difficult, and we were running out of food. Several men argued that they should be allowed to go back. I insisted that they continue. When our supplies had run out, we killed and ate some of the horses, so we wouldn't starve. We came out of the Sierras after wandering around for three weeks, and that was when we discovered the most beautiful valley in the western foothills of the Sierras. I heard they're calling it Yosemite Valley now days."

"Shucks, that's quite an exciting story," exclaimed Bill. "I will have to see that valley someday."

Later, on their way back to the wagons, Bill and Walker encountered a lone wagon. It was very dilapidated and had only a tattered covering. Its occupants were a black family.

That's one family we don't want on our wagon train, Bill thought to himself.

Walker talked to them and found out they were headed for California as well. Much to Bill's dismay, he said, "Why don't you join our wagon train?"

Later, Walker told Bill privately, "I'll bet they're runaway slaves."

"Do you really think Riker will let them join our train?"

"I don't see why not."

"Do you really think there will be a war over slavery?" Bill asked.

"It certainly is a possibility. A lot will depend on who gets elected president of the United States next."

"Which side would you be on if you have to fight?" Bill asked.

"I try to stay out of politics as much as possible. But I don't believe in slavery," Walker replied.

Riker called a meeting to discuss their new member, Duffy Washington.

Several of the members were adamant. "We don't want any black family slowing us down. Did you see the shape their wagon and team are in?"

Walker defended his position. "You would leave them to fend for themselves against this wilderness and possibly hostile natives?"

Elizabeth commented, "There, but for the grace of God, could be any of us."

The argument went on for quite a while, but Walker's decision to include the refugees finally prevailed.

Riker agreed to take his fee as wagon master out in trade.

Chapter Seven

LEARNING TO COPE

GRASS VALLEY GOLDFIELD, CALIFORNIA

AUGUST 14, 1853

Jason was still recovering, but he made time to be with the kids at their house. He, too, wanted to find out where the Swede might have hidden his gold. He was worried about how he was going to support the growing children.

"Greta, what did your pappy like to do when he wasn't digging for gold?"

"He liked to read, but he did that at nighttime."

"What kind of books did he read?"

"He called them dime evils."

Jason thought a while about what dime evil could be. Then he remembered he'd found some dime novels while cleaning up the mess the house was left in. *That must be it*, he thought. He didn't bother to correct Greta, who still did most of the talking for the two children.

"Oh, and he liked to whittle strange things out of wood," Greta continued.

"What kind of strange things?"

"Well, sometimes, he whittled sticks, so they looked like . . . well, just sticks."

Jason was puzzled over that, but that was all the information Greta volunteered in response to his questions.

Jason loved walking through the woods near his mining claim. One time, he saw a gray squirrel with a long, fluffy tail and cheeks full of acorns scamper up a nearby oak tree. The squirrel disappeared into a hole in the oak behind a short, dead branch sticking out from the tree.

From Jason's viewpoint, he couldn't see the hole itself. It looked like the squirrel had just disappeared. This gave Jason an idea. He knew many of the old oak trees in the area developed small cavities, often used by squirrels to store their winter supply of food. Some of these cavities were big enough to hide a small, leather bag of gold nuggets miners called a poke. The Swede could have whittled the branches to be plugs, to camouflage the openings of his hidey-holes in old oak trees.

Jason started his search in the woods surrounding the clearing where the Swede's cabin was built. He tested every small stub of a branch low enough to reach until finally, after over an hour of searching, he found it. A branch came away in his hand, and there it was. He dug out not one, but two small sacks of gold nuggets.

"Well, I'll be hornswoggled!" he exclaimed. That hole couldn't hold any more, but Jason wondered if there were more hidey-holes in different trees. He didn't find any more that afternoon. "But I will continue searching later," he vowed.

He took the gold nuggets he had found to work with him the next day and weighed them on Roussiere's scale.

Roussiere helped Jason figure out the value of the find. "The conversion rate of gold nowadays is $20.67 per ounce. You have 7.5 pounds, which equals 120.948 ounces . . . with sixteen ounces per pound . . . That comes to twenty-five hundred dollars."

Jason wasn't sure just what to do with the money. He was careful to not reveal where he had found the Swede's gold or that he had left it in Roussiere's safe.

He told the assembled miners that night around the campfire, "I've found what I think is the Swede's gold stash."

This announcement caused a loud clamor among the miners.

"Where did you find it?" asked Mike.

"How did you figure it out?" demanded Luke.

"I won't say where or how I found it because there very well could be more, but I want to do something for the orphaned children. I propose to build a better house for the Swede's kids to live in."

Long John seconded Jason's idea. "That sounds like a right fine use of the gold. Count me in to help with any improvements that you decide to make."

Most of the other miners agreed, except for Stephen and Luke, who strangely had little to say.

When the meeting at the campfire broke up, Stephen and Luke slunk off toward their claim, whispering together.

Luke said, "We need to keep an eye on Jason to see where that gold stash is."

"Yup," agreed Stephen. "You take first light tomorrow, and I'll spell you after a bit."

Jason had enough money from the Swede's stash to buy the lumber. He found out he'd have to travel around five miles to Nevada City in order to buy the lumber he needed for the planned expansion of the Swede's house.

At one time, there used to be two sawmills just outside of Centerville, but they were attacked and burned to the ground by natives back in 1850. The owner of one of the mills rebuilt, but the mill's prices were too high for Jason's budget. He planned a real house, with two bedrooms and closets for storage, and new furniture, like beds, and a kitchen table and chairs. He also planned a new outhouse closer to the back door where it would be more convenient, a creature comfort in the cold of night. He and some of the miners would provide the labor.

On his next day off from working at the general store, he asked Long John, "Do you mind watching the children while I ride into Nevada City to the sawmill to see about the lumber I need to expand the Swede's house?"

"It'll be my pleasure."

Jason went by the store and asked Roussiere, "Can I borrow a horse to ride to Nevada City?"

"Sure, you can make a deposit of the accumulated gold we have stocked up on your way."

As he arrived in Nevada City, he took in the rutted, dirt main street with its clapboard structures, many of them unpainted. It was the middle of the day, and the town sat as quiet as a ghost town. Everyone was away working their claims. As he traveled along, he saw many saloons, some stores, a livery stable, and many sheds, but not many homes. He assumed most of the miners lived in makeshift brush structures like his own, and other miners in Grass Valley built close to their claims. That way, they could be close to protect their claims from claim jumpers.

On his way through the city, Jason stopped off at the Wells Fargo office to drop off Roussiere's accumulated gold from the general store.

The mill was set clear on the far side of town in a clearing amongst the plentiful pine trees. A fast-running stream that turned a waterwheel ran down one side of the clearing. The waterwheel, in turn, provided the power for the mill. When Jason arrived there, he told the mill foreman of his plans.

The mill foreman explained to Jason, "It'll take about a week for the mill to get all the materials cut for what you've ordered."

"That's all right. Could you arrange to have the material delivered by wagon to Centerville to Roussiere's General Store? I'll pay half now and the rest upon delivery."

While Jason was leaving to head back to Grass Valley, he noticed several natives hanging around watching the sawmill in operation. He hoped they weren't planning on attacking this mill, like the other one in Grass Valley. He asked the mill foreman, "Why are the natives so curious about the mill?"

"They think it's magic, the way the stream provides the power to run saws. They want to know how we made friends with the Spirit of the stream."

During the week, while he waited for the lumber to arrive, Jason decided to keep a low profile. He didn't search for any more of the gold the Swede may have stashed. He wanted to be cautious and let enough time pass, so whoever else was searching for the gold would give up and go about their business. On his day off from the store, he decided to take a hunting trip. Roussiere told him he could leave the kids with him at the store, since he didn't mind watching them.

About three hours' journey west on horseback from Centerville, there was a place that Jason loved to go hunting. It was named Cache Creek. When he arrived there, he always saw eagles soaring over the valley. When he visited the valley on this hunting trip, it was raining when he got there; but under the branches of the many oak trees, he found shelter. He had always felt the presence of God in this place. He had brought a journal he'd started recently to practice his left-handed writing. While he waited for the rain to stop, he felt inspired to pen this poem:

Where the Majestic Eagles Fly

Where the majestic eagles fly,
Where the clouds forever cry,
Where the trails wind up hill,
And the views are going on still

Where Cache Creek thunders down
Far from the sight of any town
And the mighty oaks still spread
Their protecting branches overhead

Where the graceful egret sail
Over meadows, streams, and trail

Where the black bears range free
As far as the eyes can see

Where herds of elk still roam
Through the forests they call home
And the beaver builds their dams
Where natives have shaped the lands

Where the wildflowers cover the hills
And are so beautiful it gives you chills
In the springtime of the year
That you vow to return next year

Where the deer still run the range
And it doesn't seem at all strange
To see hunters braving the weather
For the glimpse of an eagle feather

Where God's plan is evident to all
And everyone can hear His call,
Where you learn to expect no less—
This is the Cache Creek wilderness.

When the rain let up, he continued his search for deer. He saw black bears roaming the hills. It was a mother with her two cubs, and Jason kept his distance. There was a herd of elk that spent the summer along the creek. But their meat was too gamey for his taste. He preferred the milder taste of deer meat. So, he moved on.

Beaver had built a dam across the creek in one place. The wildflowers grew plentifully. He found lupine, irises, poppies, and wild roses cover the hillsides. There were big trout jumping in the stream.

The Pomo tribe had a village in this valley, next to the stream. When Jason arrived at the Pomo village, he encountered Chief Wehmeh of the Nisenan tribe in Grass Valley. When he enquired what the chief was doing visiting the Pomo, Chief Wehmeh replied, "I come to hunt. No better hunting exists for many miles."

Of all the game roaming the hills here, Jason loved to hunt the deer best. He went hunting with Chief Wehmeh, and they soon spotted a large buck. Trying to shoot left-handed, Jason missed his shot, but it didn't take long before Jason and his friend got another chance.

This time, Jason downed it with one shot. He was slowly getting used to shooting left-handed, and he found out his left eye was actually his dominant eye, rather than his right eye. The chief helped him field dress the deer, since doing it one-handed was difficult, and they packed it onto the pack horse they had brought with them for that purpose.

They continued hunting so the chief could get a deer also. It didn't take long before the chief showed his skill with a bow and arrow, killing a large buck with a shot through its neck. They added this to load on the pack horse, and after the chief dropped off most of his kill back at the village, they headed back to Grass Valley.

The trip home seemed to go by fast. Chief Wehmeh accompanied Jason.

"Why did you leave most of that buck you shot with the Pomo?" Jason asked.

"Have you heard of the Bloody Island Massacre?"

"Oh, no, they weren't there, were they?"

"Yes, you know that the ranchers Kelsey and Stone were more savage than any Pomo could ever be. They not only kidnapped the Pomo people and made them work for them, but they starved them, too. They also abused their maidens, and when the maidens' parents objected, they beat them for doing so—some so severely that they died."

"Oh, I didn't know all that."

"Then when Chief Augustine couldn't stand his people being abused anymore and took revenge, the U.S. cavalry was called in. And when they could not find Chief Augustine's band, they attacked innocent women, children, and a few warriors. They slaughtered almost one hundred of the Pomo people. I only come to help provide food for the survivors whenever I can."

Jason was sympathetic toward the remains of the Pomo native tribe and told the chief, "If I'd known all that, I'd have left some of my deer for them as well."

After enough time had passed, Jason went to see if he might find more gold stashes close to the Swede's cabin and the Bloomfield Mine. Since he had a good idea it was Luke and Stephen who'd been watching him, he went by their claims first to verify they were working them before he continued his search close to that old mine.

Now that he knew what to look for, his search proved more fruitful. It took him only half an hour to find three more trees with stashes of gold. Since he couldn't be sure he wasn't being watched, Jason took the gold pokes and made a trip into town. He opened a bank account in the kids' names and put the money where it'd be safe.

The next day, while Jason worked at the general store, the wagonload of lumber arrived. Jason greeted the driver enthusiastically and asked him to wait while he got his money from Roussiere's safe to pay for the building materials. It was close to quitting time, so Roussiere told him to go ahead and take off.

"I'm sure glad you were the one to find the Swede's gold. No telling what would have happened if some of these characters around here had found it first," said Roussiere.

Jason rode with the wagon driver over to the house and helped him unload the lumber. He paid the driver and made sure to get a receipt for the amount.

His own place was next door, so the children could use it to live in temporarily while the renovations were being made to their new house.

Jason managed to get by pretty well using his left hand by now, but he knew it'd be a whole other story driving nails left-handed. He began by laying out the perimeter of the new rooms he planned to build. He found digging the holes for the corner posts was difficult, so he decided to start cutting the timber to the required lengths. He'd purchased a cross-cut saw that was small enough that he could use it one-handed. By the time he'd finished that, it was getting on to dusk, and the mosquitoes were driving him crazy. He'd had about enough of being a left-handed carpenter when Long John happened by. He was on his way home from working his claim for the day.

"So, your lumber arrived, did it? Why didn't you let us know, so we could have helped you get started?"

"Sorry about that. The lumber just arrived unannounced, and I was eager to get started. Could you round up some of our friends and help me tomorrow? I'd do it, but I have the kids to tend to."

"Sure thing. You can count on us. We'll be here bright and early tomorrow morning."

###

Jason rose early the next morning and looked in on the children. But he was surprised to find them gone. Their bed was messed, so they had slept there, but he noticed with growing panic that their clothes and few personal possessions were gone as well.

As he ran outside to start searching, Long John and his group of miners arrived to help Jason with the building construction.

Long John said, "We're here to—" Noticing Jason's panicked state, he said, "What's the matter?"

"The kids are gone. I'm glad you all are here. You can help me look for them. They slept here last night, so they couldn't have gone far. Some of you go up stream, and the rest go down stream."

As the search party spread out, they stopped by each claim and questioned those who were working panning in the creek if they had seen the kids.

Finally, Long John found one miner who had seen them. "They were headed down toward Auburn about an hour ago."

"Were they with anyone?"

"No, they were alone and on foot."

Long John sent one of the miners with him back to tell Jason; then he hurried down the road in the direction indicated and soon came upon the two runaways sitting on a log beside the road.

"Where do you think you are going?"

Greta jumped to her feet with a tear-streaked face and replied, "We were going to San Francisco to catch a ship back home."

"Don't you know this is your home now? Why, just this morning, Jason and some of us are starting to rebuild your house so it will be bigger and much better. How can Jason take care of you properly if you keep running off like this?"

When Jason reunited with the kids, he grabbed them in his arms and said, "Don't ever scare me like that again. I almost had a heart attack when I found you gone."

Chapter Eight

MAKING NEW FRIENDS

AUGUST 30, 1853

B ill had a plan. Elizabeth had complained about having to walk while the wagon train moved slowly toward California. He planned to catch and break a wild horse for his sister to ride. He'd seen many bands of wild mustangs roaming the wilderness. He'd practiced with his lasso while guarding the horses and oxen at night. Walker had been teaching him how to break and train a horse for riding.

Bill knew he still had a lot to learn about taming and training a wild horse, but from what Walker had told him, many wild horses were once domesticated. They just needed minimal training to be good mounts again. Bill often rode out on scouting trips with Walker. One day, when he was coming back with a message from Joseph for the wagon train, he topped a ridge and saw a cloud of dust approaching him in the distance. At first, he thought it was a band of natives; but as the cloud got closer, he made out individual horses, and they didn't have riders. It was a herd of wild horses.

He realized this could be the right time and place for his plans to come together. He looked around the terrain, which consisted of rolling desert sage with rocky ridges, some of which had pine trees growing along them. He soon spotted an ideal ambush place where he could get close enough to the herd to rope one of them. There were some tall rocks and scrub oaks that formed a shoot that Bill saw could work as a trap. This shoot formed the only pass over the high ridge, and the herd obviously had to use it.

He headed off the herd, and upon reaching the site, he securely tied his horse—a small but durable Morgan he'd named Spot—a safe distance away from the place he planned on catching the wild horse. He advanced on foot, hid behind a tall rock, and readied his lasso.

Belatedly, he remembered the wind. Using a trick Walker taught him, he picked up a handful of dust and slowly released it to watch which way it blew. He was in luck; the wind was coming from the same direction as the horses, so they wouldn't smell his scent and shy away from the trap.

It seemed to take forever until the herd got there. He began to think the horses took a different route. But finally, they arrived, bursting through the shoot between the rocks and pine trees. There were mustangs of all colors: tan, brown, white, black, and every combination. *I'm lucky it's the lead mare at the front with the stallion in charge at the end,* he realized. *The stallion would not have let his herd get this close to me.*

Suddenly, he saw his chance; there was a gap in the line of horses. He stepped out from his hiding place and swung his lasso, as he had practiced. It dropped neatly over the head of a pretty bay mare. But at the same time, a slim, brown figure dropped out of the tree, right onto the back of the mare. Bill was so astonished, he almost dropped the rope, but then tightened his hold again and yelled, "Hey, that's my horse!"

A young brave, about his own age, straddled the mustang. The youth hung on like a burr, even without a saddle or bridle. The horse had ideas of her own and reared up to try and dislodge her rider. Bill took a turn around a pine tree and tied off his lasso. The horse fought both the rope and her rider for a long time but finally gave up and stood trembling, with the boy still on her back. He slid off and secured his conquest with a hand on the rope. He approached Bill.

"My horse!" he claimed.

"That you're holding with my rope!" Bill responded, with more than a little animosity.

The adversaries eyed each other with determined looks for a long couple of moments.

Bill suddenly relaxed his stance, then said, "We make a good team. How about you keep this one and help me catch another one?"

The native boy thought a moment. Then he relaxed, too, and asked, "You with wagon train?"

"Yes," Bill answered, a little concerned that the native was aware of the train moving through his land.

"Why you need another horse? You have many horses!"

Really concerned now, Bill answered, "This horse was to be for my sister, who has to walk all day." He admired the necklace of bear's claws the youth was wearing around his neck. Then he asked, "How do you know English so well?"

"I learn at Mission School."

The two young men soon became fast friends united by a common cause of catching and taming wild mustangs. Bill learned the young brave was a Choctaw and that a Choctaw's wealth was measured by the number of horses he owned. His name was Luca Nita.

Bill asked, "What does Luca Nita translate to?"

"Luca Nita means 'black bear.' When I was come home from becoming man, we meet and kill black bear in woods. So, my father give me new name for new man I become. These are from that bear." He fingered his necklace.

Bill asked, "Do you have a big family?"

"Me have two little sisters, both at home. My father's brothers have many children my age. What they called in English?"

"Cousins."

Over the next few weeks, Bill had several opportunities to meet Luca Nita, as the horse hunting conveniently followed the same trail as the wagon train. He learned a lot from his new friend about catching and taming wild horses. Bill managed to keep his liaison with the youth a secret from his sister or any of the other members of the wagon train—until he finally gave the green-broke mustang to Elizabeth, and she demanded to know where it came from. When she learned her baby brother had matured enough to disregard conventional bigotries and make friends with a native boy, she was actually proud to be his sister.

###

The wagon train was driving through a dry wash with sparse vegetation. Everyone pulled up their bandanas that they all wore around their necks to keep out the choking dust. Elizabeth was driving their wagon because Bill had gone scouting with Walker. Esther was riding on the wagon seat next to her. She decided to use the time to give Esther a beginning geography lesson.

"Now, Esther," Elizabeth shouted through her bandana, "where are we going on this wagon train?"

Esther didn't say anything. She just shrugged her little shoulders.

Elizabeth said, "California is where we're going. Can you say California?"

"Ca—i—for—a." She gave it a good try.

"Very good, Esther," she encouraged her student. Any response was progress.

That evening in camp, the pioneers were joined by travelers coming east. Elizabeth was eager to learn what was happening in the world outside of the wagon train. While around the campfire, she asked them, "What city did you just come through?"

"Albuquerque, young lady. It isn't an official city just yet, but it will be soon."

"What news was there on those Southern states who were threatening secession from the Union?"

"Well, young lady, there were rumors of close to a dozen Southern states threatening secession, but I don't think President Fillmore will let things go that far."

A bystander made the remark, "If they do, it will mean a war." This comment started a heated discussion around the campfire that went on for hours.

"I say, let them go if they wanna." This was from an obvious Northerner.

"But without the blacks, who would pick our crops? All the plantations would go bust."

"That's no reason for slavery. Can you stand there and tell me it's right to enslave a whole race just because of the color of their skin?"

"The war, if it comes, will be to preserve the Union, not to free the slaves," another Northern sympathizer said.

"It should be the right of any state to leave the Union if they wanna."

Finally, Riker had to step in and end the argument. "We have an early start in the morning, so let's break it up and get some rest."

The following evening, Bill sat next to the Sterling wagon with Susan. He was courting his new friend. He was also spying on Bob Sterling for his sister. Inside the wagon, they could hear Bob talking with Esther.

"When we find a place to settle down, we will have a new home, and you will have a new mother."

Bill perked up and listened even closer. He heard Esther ask, "Who will be my new mother?"

"How would you like to have Elizabeth for your new mom?" her father asked.

"I like Elizabeth," Esther replied with enthusiasm.

Bill thought, *Well, now, that's interesting. I'll have to tell Elizabeth about this.*

One night, there was a full moon that spread silvery light over the landscape. Bill saw Susan and Steward slip away from the circled wagons. He followed them and got close enough to hear their murmuring voices, and then he heard the unmistakable sound of an angry hand slapping someone's face. Bill immediately burst through the bushes to where Susan was yelling at a departing Steward.

"Don't you ever try that again," she yelled. But when she saw Bill, her anger turned to relief. "Oh, Bill, thank goodness it's you."

"What did he do?"

"Oh, well, he just tried to steal a kiss."

Bill stared at the fiery, redheaded, young woman before him, blazing with indignation. He didn't blame Steward; truth be told, he wanted to steal a kiss from Susan, too. He started to go after Steward, but Susan restrained him.

"Don't go. I'd much rather enjoy the moonlight with you."

Bill couldn't resist such an invitation. He stared at the lovely, young woman in front of him. He longed to run his hands through the mass of red curls that framed her delicate face and kiss those ruby red lips.

Suddenly, Susan was in Bill's arms. He didn't know how she got there, but he held her close, relishing the feel of her body enclosed in his arms.

After a while, they drew apart and looked into each other's eyes. Slowly, Susan rose on her tip toes and brought her mouth closer to Bill's. When their lips finally met, it was all over for Bill. He realized this was the one he wanted to spend the rest of his life with. As they walked hand-in-hand back to Susan's wagon, Bill said a silent prayer. *Thank you, Lord, for bringing Susan into my life.*

Later that night, Elizabeth was sitting around the campfire with Esther. At first, Elizabeth had to have Bob with her when she talked with Esther; she was so shy and needed the reassurance of her father's presence. Gradually, over time, Esther got to know and trust Elizabeth, and Elizabeth could work with her alone. This evening, Esther was sitting at the other end of the log from Elizabeth. Esther still had problems being shy and withdrawn around other people. She seemed to be having trouble adjusting to her pappy being her only parent. Unfortunately, her father was not the nurturing or affectionate type. He was a good provider, but he busied himself with more important matters.

Now, for instance, he was in a heated discussion with John Riker and Joseph Walker. They were debating whether to take the Cimarron Cutoff or continue through the Mountain Branch of the Santa Fe Trail.

Walker was pressing for the Cimarron Cutoff. "I've been both ways, and the Cimarron Cutoff is shorter by nearly one hundred miles. It also avoids going over Raton Pass, which is almost impassable for wagons."

Riker was pushing to use the Mountain Branch. He said, "What about that fifty-mile section of dry plain?"

Walker replied, "I came back that way, and there was plenty of water."

"That was several months ago; are you sure the water is still there?" asked Sterling.

Riker added, "The Mountain Branch leads to that new trail that goes along the Purgatoire River. It is much easier for wagons, and we don't have to worry about water."

Water access being a priority, this settled the argument, and they decided to take the Mountain Branch and try the Purgatoire River route.

"Esther, what do you want to be when you grow up?" Elizabeth asked.

"I don't know; maybe a teacher like you."

Elizabeth's face flushed with pleasure that the child thought enough of Elizabeth to want to be like her. "That would be nice, Esther, but there are several other things you can be."

"Are you going to be my new mommy?"

Wondering where that came from, Elizabeth replied, "I haven't been asked to be your mother. Where did you get that idea?"

"My daddy said we need a new mommy, and you fit the bill."

That certainly gave Elizabeth food for thought. "I would love to be your mommy, but . . ." *What should I say?* "Well, honey, I am already promised to someone waiting for me in California." She left it at that.

Elizabeth made herself spend more time with Esther. She found out from talking to the child's father that the six-year-old had changed drastically since her mother's death. She had become extremely shy and depressed, woke up at nights with bad dreams, and didn't interact with others well.

Elizabeth found that just spending time with her seemed to help most of all. Elizabeth didn't have any special training for troubled children, but she loved all children and was instinctively drawn to those with problems. Her teacher's training involved role-playing.

"Now, Esther, I've made you dolls to play with. Here, take them and play whatever you like."

Elizabeth had made the dolls resemble Esther, along with her mother and father. She had gotten Esther's mother's description from conversations with Bob. At first, Esther only wanted to play with the doll that was like her. She seemed to shy away from the father doll, and she completely ignored the mother doll.

But finally, one day, Elizabeth observed her pick up the doll resembling her mother. She held it close for a while, and then she laid it down on its back. She observed it for a while with a sad expression, and then Elizabeth noticed tears running down the little girl's face. Elizabeth instinctively wanted to hold Esther and comfort her, but for some reason, she didn't. She waited, and finally, Esther resumed playing with the doll resembling herself.

After that incident, Esther seemed to act more like a typical six-year-old. It was as if she had dealt with the death of her mother and moved on. Elizabeth continued to spend quality time with Esther. She liked the way Esther was becoming attached to her, but she wondered about what would happen once the journey ended and they went their separate ways.

On September 10, 1853, the Riker wagon train camped one night at a sight across the river from the former Bent's Fort. William Bent had built his unique fort on the northern bank of the Arkansas River.

Bill had heard so much about this, he convinced Walker to take him across the river to visit the site.

When they arrived there, Bill remarked, "Wow, I see now why Bent chose this site."

The remains of the fort overlooked a splendid view of the Spanish Peaks, Pike's Peak, and the flowing valley of the Arkansas River.

Walker told Bill, "Back in '33, when the Bent brothers built this fort, it was the grandest fort on the frontier. It had solid, adobe walls thirty inches thick and fourteen feet or more high. There were twenty-five large sleeping rooms. There were warehouses, a kitchen, a dining hall, a blacksmith, and a carpentry shop."

"There are so many stories about what happened to make William Bent blow up his fort. You said you stayed here several times. What really happened?" asked Bill.

"Well, it was a combination of several things. Both of his brothers died within a year. The youngest brother had been killed by natives back in 1841. The Mexican-American War ruined the trading business. Bent's friendship with his partner Saint Vrain fell apart. In '49, all the gold-seekers passed through, leaving behind a cholera epidemic that wiped out half of the Cheyenne tribe that had given William two wives and a number of children. At the same time, the Ute, Apache, Comanche, and even Arapaho were threatening to attack the fort. The U.S. government offered a mere fifteen thousand dollars to buy the fort.

"Suddenly, it all seemed too much. William ordered everyone out of the fort and had everything moved five miles away down river. He then rode back and blew it up after setting fire to the wood structures." Walker turned back to the camp. "Come on, Bill. Let's go get some supper."

Bill and Susan were getting along quite well. Since his rescue of her at the Arkansas River crossing and the moonlight meeting, the two had been inseparable. They ate their meals together, often prepared by Susan, who was quite a cook. When Bill wasn't riding his horse, they walked together and learned all about each other.

Elizabeth, who admittedly was not much of a cook herself, started learning from Susan. Currently, she watched Susan prepare what she called "Spotted Pup." The ingredients were one cup of rice, two cups of water, a handful of raisins, a little molasses, cinnamon to taste, and one tablespoon of vanilla.

Susan said, "Preparation is simple. Just put everything into a pot and bring it to a boil."

Elizabeth tasted the finished dish and exclaimed, "Why, this is delicious just as it is."

"Yup, or it can be used as a topping," Susan said.

When the meal was ready, Susan asked Bill to say the blessing.

"Lord, bless this food and thank You for safe traveling so far on our journey. Be with Joseph Walker and Mr. Riker so that they lead us all safely to California. Amen."

Susan liked that Bill was also a spiritual man. It was just what she wanted for her husband.

But Bill couldn't be with Susan all the time. He spent some of his time scouting with Walker. When he was gone, Steward took advantage of it and tried to get close to Susan.

"What do you see in that Bill fella?" Steward asked Susan. They were walking to the side of the wagons to be out of the dust.

"What's not to like? Did you see that nice horse he caught and tamed for his sister? He also saved me from drowning back in the Arkansas River crossing."

"Well, I heard he's friends with one of those stinkin' natives."

"There are good natives as well as bad ones. Just like there are good white men as well as bad white men," Susan replied.

What could Steward say to that?

"I forgot to mention it," said Bill to Elizabeth as they took a stroll together, "but I overheard Bob Sterling telling Esther that he plans on having you for her new mom."

"Goodness, then it's true what Joseph Walker and Esther said."

"What are you gonna do about it, Lizzy?"

"I love Esther already, but I don't love him—not like I do Jason, at least. I'll just pray about it and hope God works things out . . . somehow."

Chapter Nine

THE PLOT THICKENS

GRASS VALLEY GOLDFIELD, CALIFORNIA

SEPTEMBER 5, 1853

The additions to the Swede's old cabin for the kids weren't taking nearly as long as Jason thought they would. In fact, they were nearly completed, thanks to one of the miners by the name of Shorty.

He had been a farmer in his former life, and he came up with the idea. "Why don't you do the addition like a barn-raising?

Jason asked, "How would that be?"

"We build each wall lying flat on the ground, and then we tip them up one at a time."

They took Shorty's advice, and after the walls were framed, the ten miners helping Jason, tipped them up, one at a time, and secured them to the corner posts. After that, it was short work to finish them off, both outside and inside. The hole for the new outhouse was dug, and the outhouse was moved and put in place. Then they put on the roofing for the main house. The floor was still dirt, but Jason found he had some two-by-six planks left over, which were enough to put down rough floors, for the two bedrooms.

During this time, Jason spent many hours trying to figure out why God had let this accident happen to him. He had always tried to do the right thing and believed that good comes to those that did. He had never had trouble praying to God. However, since the accident, he felt more like God had abandoned him. It worried him, too, that he didn't know what Elizabeth would make of his loss of faith, since she was a good, God-fearing Christian. He didn't know, for that matter, what she would make of his loss of his right hand. That bothered him just about as much as his loss of faith. He felt a little guilty for not writing and telling her about his accident.

Jason had saved up some gold on his own before his accident, but he'd used up a good portion of it since then to just get by. But if he combined what was left of it with what he had found of the Swede's, it totaled quite a sum.

Jason and Long John were sitting on a boulder overlooking Wolf Creek. The two comrades didn't say much, but these thoughts ran through Jason's head. Finally, he said to Long John, "My original plan, of course, was to send for Elizabeth when I had acquired enough to give us a good start. Now, however, I don't have enough of a stake to send for her. And I'm unsure how Elizabeth will react to me being a cripple."

"If she's any kind of Christian woman, she will stand by you, even with your little handicap."

I'm glad one of us still has their faith, anyway, thought Jason.

Roussiere gave Jason more and more time at the general store. He'd taught Jason every aspect of the business. He often complained that his wife constantly nagged him to quit the goldfield and return to Boston.

One day, as Jason was sweeping up, he told Jason, "If I had a buyer, I would sell the store and head back east."

Just out of curiosity, Jason asked, "How much would you be asking?"

Roussiere named a sum that was well within his means, if he used his personal stake of accumulated gold.

This was a drastic change in Jason's original plans. Being a cautious man, he told Roussiere, "I might just be interested in buying you out, but let me think on it. Is it okay if I let you know?"

"How is Jason getting along?" asked Marcos Wilson, who had just happened upon Long John's mining claim.

"He's slowly learning to live with his disability," replied Long John. "He's learned to use his left hand almost as well as his right for most things. He still has trouble writing. His new signature when doing so looks nothing like his old right-handed signature. He's spent hours practicing until his frustration gets the better of him."

"Has he told his fiancée about the accident?"

"I don't think he has written to Elizabeth since the accident. He still has doubts about her reaction to his accident and being a cripple."

"It takes time to adjust. I've seen much worse," admitted Marcos. "But from what he's told me about his fiancée, I have a feeling that she will love him just as he is."

"We'll certainly pray to that end," replied Long John. "A man needs a good woman by his side—especially when his life has been upended. And those children sure could use a mother."

"Indeed. Well, I best be moving along. I have some other claims to check in on."

With concern for Jason weighing heavily on his mind, Long John went back to work as his friend went on his way.

Jason and Long John were strolling through the woods just outside Grass Valley.

"I've been thinking about what you said about God never leaving me," said Jason. "I've tried to reconnect with Him, but it doesn't seem to be working very well."

Long John said, "Why don't we pray about this together, Jason?"

Jason dubiously went along with him. They bowed their heads, and Long John prayed, "Lord, You know how Jason is struggling. You have promised to help your children through their troubles. Please draw near to Jason and strengthen him for his journey ahead. Let him know Your plan for his life and give him the strength to live it Your way. Amen."

"That was a great prayer, Long John. Where did you learn to pray like that? Are you sure you weren't a preacher before?"

"Well, you found me out, Jason. I used to be a preacher back in Illinois. But my entire congregation got the gold fever and then left for California. My wife passed away. I moped around for a while; then I thought if I couldn't beat them, why not join them? So, here I am."

Jason said, "I'm sorry about your late wife." He used to marvel at God's handiwork in nature, but he had trouble seeing God at work so much anymore. Even so, he still loved the wild beauty of the area, living among the oaks and pine trees in Grass Valley, when he disregarded the destruction and debris left behind by mining.

Although Jason was sold on placer mining as the least harmful to God's nature, he had studied other methods of mining, including hard rock mining, where gold had to be extracted from quartz rock formations. He knew this was where the big money was.

He also was familiar with various modern mining devices like the turbine engine. He knew from his engineering studies that in 1849, James B. Francis had improved the inward flow reaction turbine to over ninety percent efficiency. Jason predicted it would remain the most widely used water turbine invented.

Jason's claim on Wolf Creek was small and unobtrusive. He contemplated how he used to pan for gold. He did not leave any trace behind. He didn't see why most of the miners were so greedy for gold that they destroyed nature in the process. He scooped up sand and gravel from the stream bed in his gold pan. He swished the pan around to separate the layers. He carefully dumped the top layer of sand and gravel from his pan back into the stream. He examined the remaining base layer of sediment in his pan for gold specks. If they existed, he carefully removed the gold dust that remained and stored it in his poke. He dumped the rest of the sediment back into the stream and then started all over again.

Now, with only one good hand, he scooped up a pan full of gravel with his good left hand; then he swished it around to separate the layers and carefully dumped off the top layer. Next, he wedged the pan between his body and right arm, which now had the fake, wooden hand carved by Adam. He carefully picked out any gold flecks left in the bottom sediment layer. Then he fumbled for his poke to store the gold in, usually dropping the pan—or worse yet, the gold—back into the stream. After this happened repeatedly, too many times to count, Jason made a decision. *It's impossible to mine one-handed. I do believe I'll take Roussiere up on his offer and buy his general store.*

Later that evening, Jason overheard Long John talking to the kids as they played with the kittens. "Greta and Sven, who would you like to live with and have take care of you?"

They both answered in unison, "Papa Jason."

Long John looked over his shoulder and winked at Jason standing by the doorway. He said, "Nothing like having a purpose."

The way Jason figured it, he was the kids' new guardian. He was looking into legally adopting them, since they had no relatives in America. It was up to him to make decisions that were in their best interest. Running the store would give him a better opportunity to be a proper parent than being a miner.

He knew Elizabeth would support his decision, since she loved children and had expressed the desire to have a large family. He had grown to love the kids, and his heart went out especially to Sven and how he was suffering the loss of both his parents. He gathered them together that very night and told them of his decision.

"I've decided to use some of my gold to buy the general store. Also, I've decided to adopt you two and take care of you from now on."

They immediately ran into Jason's arms, and a long group hug ensued. Jason could tell Greta and Sven felt a big sense of relief. All the children were interested in was that he loved them and would be there to take care of them from now on.

Chapter Ten

NATIVE TROUBLE

NEW MEXICO TERRITORY

SEPTEMBER 10, 1853

E lizabeth was waist-deep in a small river about halfway between Albuquerque and El Paso. She was off by herself for a much-needed bath. It was only mid-afternoon. The wagon master had called an early halt for the day, and she was enjoying the refreshing coolness of the stream.

Suddenly, she heard a splash in the water behind her. Before she could turn to see what caused it, a strong, brown arm circled her waist, and a hand clamped over her mouth. She struggled with all her might, but her captor was much stronger. Suddenly, the hand over her mouth was released, and Elizabeth drew in a breath to scream; but it was cut off when she received a blow to the head and sunk into unconsciousness.

Sometime later, Tishomingo, Elizabeth's captor, was riding his horse to the top of a ridge. *This white eye squaw will make an interesting addition to my many wives. My scouting trip to check on the wagon train has proved more fruitful than I'd hoped.*

He had taken precautions to hide his trail well, so he wasn't worried about any pursuers from the wagon train catching up too fast. He was alone and only had the horse he was riding. He was tired of holding the unconscious prisoner across the horse in front of him.

If only I could find another horse to transport my new, captive wife. He'd taken the white woman east toward his tribe's present camp. He paused at the top of the ridge and saw dust from someone or something traveling in the valley below. He decided to investigate and took a rocky trail down into the valley. As he drew closer, he could tell it was a herd of horses making the dust.

Luca Nita, Bill's Choctaw native friend, was herding a band of wild horses. Tishomingo recognized Luca Nita and his band as they had had many run-ins with the chief of the rival Chickasaw tribe.

Luca Nita pulled up his mount and confronted Tishomingo. "What does Tishomingo want?" he demanded in greeting.

"That pinto you are riding will do," replied the chief, reacting to Luca Nita's belligerent tone of voice with attitude of his own.

This got Luca Nita's temper up. "I have spent many hours catching and taming this pony. It's worth many pelts." He noticed one of the white man's steel knives stuck into the chief's belt. It was a rare thing among his tribe. He added, "I see you have a steel knife, a rare possession indeed. I will trade this pony for that white man's knife," he added in a conciliatory tone.

Tishomingo considered the matter and finally relented, seeing he did not intimidate the Choctaw youth. Allowing his success to get the best of him, the chief didn't notice when Luca Nita followed him a short way to another ridge, noting which direction the chief was headed with his new horse.

The first thing Elizabeth felt when she finally awoke was a terrible headache. As the pounding in her head subsided somewhat, she tried to sit up but realized her hands were tied. Looking through the branches of the shelter she was under, she saw a smoldering campfire and a small stack of firewood. The rest of the camp was deserted—no horses, no sign of her captor, nothing. She was alone. The quiet stillness stole over her, and goosebumps tickled her arms. All she had on was what she'd been bathing in—her damp chamise and bloomers.

Meanwhile, Elizabeth desperately struggled with the ties binding her hands and feet. Her hands were tied behind her back, but she noticed the ties on her feet were rawhide strips, not hemp rope. This gave her hope because she knew if she got rawhide wet, it would stretch. She had a good sense of hearing, and in the quiet of the afternoon, she thought she could hear a stream in the distance.

She rolled out of the shelter and toward the sounds of the stream. She avoided as many of the sharp rocks as she could but couldn't miss all of them. Squirming through the sagebrush, she finally arrived at the edge of a ravine. She could hear the stream running at the bottom. She paused a moment and said a little prayer to herself under her breath. "Dear Jesus, please help me to get down to this stream safely."

She rolled off the bank and aimed toward some bushes growing at the stream's edge, hoping they would cushion her descent down the steep slope. It worked, almost. She felt the bushes slow her fall, but her momentum was such that she burst through them and landed in the stream. Her head hit a rock, and she blacked out again.

Her first sensation when she came to was the coolness of the running water on her face. Her head was half submerged in the stream. She couldn't tell how long she had been out, but her head now throbbed in two places. Luckily, her hair had cushioned the latest blow to her head.

She sat up and tried to see where she had landed but everything was blurry, and she almost fell over again from the dizziness. When her head cleared, she saw that the stream was very shallow at that point. She twisted her hands behind her and noticed that the rawhide bindings had indeed stretched and were much looser. Straining to free herself, she ignored the pain in her head and all over her body from the fall down into the ravine. She was rewarded for all her efforts a moment later when her hands slipped out of the ties. *Thank You, Lord.*

With her hands free, it was an easy matter to untie her feet. She stood up shakily in the stream. She decided to stay in the stream as long as possible to hide her trail. But should she head upstream or downstream? She remembered some of the survival lessons she had heard from Joseph Walker. She knew the wagon train was camped next to a river, and Walker said streams led to rivers. It'd be easier going downstream. She was still weak and unsteady on her feet, so she headed downstream.

After a short time, she felt better, and she started thinking straighter. It would be natural for her captor, whoever he was, to look for her downstream. So, she turned around and headed upstream. She hoped to confuse her captor that way. And as an added ploy, when she turned around, she discarded the rawhide strips on the side of the stream.

Her strength returned as she went. She kept on the lookout for a large section of solid rock where she could exit the stream without leaving a trail. After what seemed like a mile, she found what she sought. A large section of granite provided her a pathway up from the stream.

She had no idea where she was or how long she had been unconscious. But the sun was low on the horizon, so she assumed it was the evening of the same day. All she was concerned with at the present was putting as much distance between herself and her captor as possible. She listened closely for signs of pursuit, but all she heard were the birds in the brush that was growing up the slope she was scaling.

Finally, she topped a ridge and saw a larger stream flowing through a rocky ravine. She didn't see a way down to cross over the stream, so she headed along the ravine. Again, she questioned which way to go. Then she noted which way the larger stream flowed and headed that way, remembering what Walker had said about following downstream to a river.

###

Tishomingo rode back into his campsite leading his newly acquired horse to discover his captive had escaped. Furious, he kicked apart the shelter that had housed Elizabeth, and then he started searching the area for signs indicating which way she'd gone. It didn't take him long to find her trail leading to the ravine and down to the stream. He followed the trail downstream first and soon discovered the rawhide strips he'd used to bind her. This gave him a direction, so he went back and broke camp; and taking both horses, he headed downstream.

The sun was directly overhead when the stream he was following merged with a larger stream. He stopped to water his horses; and when he was done, he looked across the larger stream and low and behold, he saw a white woman wading out of the stream on the other shore. He mounted his horse, and letting out a war whoop, he splashed across the stream. Before Elizabeth could reach safety, he leaned down from his horse and grabbed her by her hair.

Elizabeth screamed, and then she was pulled off her feet. Her captor dismounted and secured her once again.

Bill was beginning to worry about his sister. It was almost dusk, and she hadn't returned from her bath in the nearby stream. He went to investigate and found her dress and a sweater. At first, he panicked, looking around frantically, fearing his sister had drowned. He called out, "Elizabeth, where are you?" When there was no response, he ran back to the wagon train and sounded the alarm.

Riker, Sterling, and Walker came with Bill to examine the area around the stream. Walker and Bill examined the tracks.

Riker asked, "What do you make of these tracks, Joseph?"

"It looks to me like Elizabeth was taken by only one person. They were headed east on one horse. I can tell that much from how deep the horse tracks were going out compared to the tracks coming in."

"Good. Now, Bill, how long ago did Elizabeth leave for the stream?"

Riker interrupted and said, "I wish I could go with you to find Elizabeth, but I have to finish getting the wagon train settled in for the night. You all go and follow the trail. You three should be enough against one person."

Bill was so eager to find his sister that he got ahead of Walker before they could get an answer from him. He started out on foot, and Walker had to call him back.

"Now, don't be messing up the trail, Bill," Walker cautioned the eager youth. "And don't you think we'll need our horses?"

Bill was a little embarrassed, but he took the time to go back to the wagon train and got their mounts.

Bob Sterling was sulking at the delay, and he directed his animosity at Bill. He was not the adventurous type, but he was genuinely concerned for Elizabeth because he had plans to marry her. It was getting dark fast, and Bill and Walker were losing the trail.

Walker was just about to call the search off for the night when they spotted a campfire. "Sterling, you and Bill stay back with the horses while I investigate that camp."

"I'm going," insisted Bill. "I'll be quiet, I promise."

Walker relented and said, "Okay, but stay behind me."

They made their way silently through the sagebrush and chaparral to within thirty feet of the camp, then knelt down behind some boulders. Bill peeked over the top of a boulder; then he whispered to the scout, "That's a friend of mine, a Choctaw named Luca Nita. He couldn't have kidnapped Elizabeth."

Walker didn't know what to say about this development. He whispered back, "Are you sure?" He took another peek over the boulders and said, "I don't see any captive, just some horses."

Bill stood up and approached the camp with Walker trailing behind him.

Sure enough, the young brave greeted Bill like a long-lost brother.

"What are you doing out here at night?" Luca Nita asked, eying Walker suspiciously.

"My sister, Elizabeth, has been kidnapped, and we are trailing them."

"So, that what Tishomingo was doing out here and why he needed another horse."

Walker joined in the conversation. "Do you mean Chief Tishomingo of the Chickasaw?"

"Yes, he trade for one of my horses but not say what he need it for."

Bill's face lit up in the glow of the campfire as he asked eagerly, "Do you know where his camp is?"

"No, I only see which way Tishomingo go, but he may have made false trail."

Walker said, "All we can do is camp here tonight and try getting an early start in the morning. With any luck, we can pick up his trail and catch up tomorrow." He left to bring in Sterling while Bill talked some more with his friend.

The next morning, Bill and Walker were up early, but Luca Nita beat them both. He returned to camp with the news. "I've found a small box canyon where we can leave my horses, while we go to rescue Elizabeth."

Walker asked Luca Nita, "Are you sure you want to help find Tishomingo?"

"Tishomingo is a Chickasaw. No friend of the Choctaw," he replied, as he slashed his hand down in defiance.

They took some time to secure the canyon entrance with downed trees and boulders, and all the while, Bob fumed at the additional delay. Then they set out in the direction Luca Nita had seen Tishomingo heading the day before. With the combined tracking skills of the native, Bill, and the scout, they soon found the trail and started following it. It didn't take them long to find Tishomingo's first campsite. Walker examined it closely and said to the others, "It looks to me like they camped here for a short time yesterday. This campsite isn't fresh enough for them to have left it this morning."

Luca Nita had been examining the surrounding area while Walker concentrated on the campsite itself. He called to the others, "These signs are of someone being dragged or maybe dragging themselves from that destroyed shelter over here to this gully."

Walker, Sterling, and Bill approached the bank of the gully where Luca Nita stood. As they looked down, Walker pointed and said, "Look, there where the bushes are trampled down. Someone, probably Elizabeth, must have fallen from here down to that stream."

They all descended to the stream and tried to read any signs of what happened next. Bill and Sterling went downstream, while Walker and Luca Nita went upstream. Luca Nita soon saw the tracks from Tishomingo's horses, left when he was trailing Elizabeth's false trail downstream. He called to the others, and they were soon closing the distance to the Chickasaw's second campsite.

It was morning, and Elizabeth was scared. *So far, other than the blow on my head when I was first taken and being dragged by my hair, I've been very lucky to be unharmed. I've heard numerous stories around the wagon train campfire about captive women being raped and beaten by the natives.* She heard her captor stirring around, getting ready to break camp. She shoved the animal skin blanket off herself. *I sure hope someone from the wagon train is on my trail. I'll stall as long as possible in bed to give whoever is following me more of a chance to catch up. I don't know what I'll do if Bill or Walker don't come to my rescue.* She pulled the blanket back over herself and pretended to be sleeping when her captor came to check on her. Finally, Tishomingo got tired of her stalling, and he pulled her out and shouted in a gruff tone, "Get ready; we leaving."

By this time, Joseph Walker and his band of rescuers had tracked Elizabeth and her captor to their campsite and huddled to make a plan. He cautioned everyone, "Watch out. Don't endanger Elizabeth when we attack. Spread out, so we have every side covered."

Bob Sterling saw this as his opportunity to impress Elizabeth, but to do that, he had to seem to be the one rescuing her. Seeing Tishomingo dragging Elizabeth out and throwing her on his newly acquired horse, Sterling jumped the gun, and he stepped out of hiding and fired hastily, missing his target. Tishomingo reacted quickly, raised the rifle already in his hand, and fired at Sterling. More shots rang out from three sides. Tishomingo moved quickly to get to his own mount, and the confusion caused most of the shots to miss their marks.

Bill hesitated with his shot because Elizabeth was in front of Tishomingo. When he fired, he pulled up, and his shot was high. Luca Nita fired as well; but Tishomingo was moving so fast, his shot missed, too. Walker took careful aim and hit Tishomingo. He was wounded in the shoulder. The Chickasaw realized he was outnumbered but managed to get to his horse and mount up. He kicked his horse into a gallop and headed north.

Elizabeth's green-broke horse spooked at the gunfire and took off heading south, with her barely clinging to its mane. Her hands were bound in front of her again, and the horse's panicked gate did nothing to help her stay on.

Luca Nita got to his horse first, but in his haste, he released Bill and Bob's horses. He had to decide. Should he chase after the fleeing Chickasaw, try to recover the horses, or should he try to rescue Elizabeth on the runaway horse?

Walker made the decision for him as he vaulted onto his mount. "We have to go after Elizabeth," he shouted.

Luca Nita and Walker pursued the fleeing horse with Elizabeth barely clinging on for dear life. She wasn't used to riding a horse without a saddle. Walker gained on Elizabeth with Luca Nita close behind when suddenly, Elizabeth's horse encountered a fallen log across its path. The horse jumped over the log, but Elizabeth lost her precarious balance and fell off. She landed hard on the downed tree across the trail. Her pursuers pull up to assist her.

Elizabeth was unconscious, and Walker saw, as he rolled her over, she had landed on a sharp, broken branch protruding from the tree. "She's got a serious wound in her stomach. Let's try to stop the bleeding and get her back to the wagon train to see the doc."

Luca Nita helped them rig up a travois for transporting the unconscious woman. It consisted of two long, thin poles with a blanket stretched between them to form a stretcher. The ends of the poles were tied to one of the horses, so Elizabeth was pulled along.

Bill rode up with his face drained of color and broke the news to the rest of the rescue party. "I'm afraid Sterling didn't make it. Tishomingo must have shot him in the first volley."

Bill was so shaken, his hands trembled as he helped tie the body onto his horse to take back with them.

Luca Nita said, "You not need me now. I return to my horses."

When they arrived back at the wagon train, Walker said, "Bill, go find the doctor."

Bill arrived back with the doctor and implored him, "You have to help her, Doc. She didn't deserve something like this. She hasn't regained consciousness since she fell off the horse."

Doc Freeman, a retired doctor traveling to California, completed his examination, bandaged her wound, and gave her something to make her sleep, which she did for the rest of that evening and night.

###

The next morning, Elizabeth awoke. "Tell me where it hurts," the doctor said.

Elizabeth clutched her stomach.

"The primary damage seems to be here, to the pelvic area. Does this hurt?" he asked his patient as he probed the area.

"Ow," Elizabeth groaned in response to the doctor's probing. "What happened? How did I get here?" she asked.

"You're a very lucky lady," Walker replied. "You fell from your horse, and we brought you back here on that travois contraption Luca Nita rigged up."

Doctor Freeman said, "I think you'll be okay. Can you sit up?"

Elizabeth tried but fell back with another groan.

"You have a puncture wound that will limit your activities for a while. You have to rest in bed until you're better."

Bob Sterling's death impacted more than his orphaned child. Elizabeth and Bill were also affected. They felt responsible somehow.

Riker was questioning them early one morning. "Does Esther have any relatives we should notify?"

Elizabeth answered, "Not that we know of. Bob didn't have any brothers or sisters, and his parents just passed away recently. Esther's mother didn't have any relatives close by, either. We will be responsible for Esther."

That evening, there was a solemn ceremony beside a hastily dug grave in a grove of aspen trees. Riker read a verse from his Bible.

Esther wept for the loss of her father. But everyone knew that the wagon train could not stay there. They had to keep moving.

It was a few weeks later, and Elizabeth had taken it easy resting in the wagon as they continued their journey west. Doctor Freeman had completed a follow-up examination on Elizabeth and pronounced, "You are free to resume normal activities as you feel able."

Elizabeth had tried to do just that, but when she had tried riding her new horse, she suffered a relapse. Doctor Freeman performed a more thorough exam this time. He determined that she had an infection and told her, "You have to be on bedrest again. The worst thing that you may suffer from this type of injury is you may not be able to have babies."

Elizabeth didn't let on to the doctor, but his pronouncement hurt very much because one of her fondest wishes was to have a big family with Jason. *Please, Lord, don't let it be so. You know Jason and I want to have children. We've planned all along to have a big family, and now this. It's not fair, Lord.* She cried herself to sleep that night.

Susan came by one evening while Elizabeth was still recuperating from her accident. "We all miss you, Elizabeth. When will you be well enough to ride that horse Bill caught and tamed for you?"

"I miss you, too. The doc has cleared me, so I hope to get out and do some walking this next week. It will probably be another week before I can ride."

"Have you named your horse yet?"

"Yes, I've named her Buttercup. She is such a sweetheart."

"My dad says Bill did a great job taming that horse for you. He should know. He used to work in a livery stable back in Jackson."

"Is that where you're from?"

"Yes, born and raised in Missouri. We had a farm at first, just outside of town, but we had a drought that lasted five years, and Father had to take a job in town to make ends meet."

"When did you decide to head for California?"

"Father has been reading all those stories in the newspaper about striking it rich in the California goldfields. Finally, he just got fed up with scraping by, barely making it. And one day, he told Mother and me, 'Pack up everything essential; I have a wagon someone left at the livery. We're headin' for California.' We didn't argue much. We were fed up, too."

Susan stayed for a while to keep Elizabeth company and then said goodnight before heading back to her own wagon. As she walked under the night sky, she said a prayer for her friend, asking that her recovery would be quick and complete.

He had made a big decision. Luca Nita had decided to stay with the wagon train for a while. He convinced Riker to trade for some of his herd of horses, so he was well-supplied. Some of Luca Nita's Choctaw friends came to see what the attraction was at the wagon train. They knew he was thinking of joining the train.

Luca Nita's cousin, Chebona Bula, asked him, "Why do you wish to join the white man and travel to a far land?"

"Me like to see new places and learn new things. This my chance to do that. John Riker, the chief of the wagon train, has offered me a job scouting and hunting wild horses. These things I know how to do well. He will pay for this with food and shelter."

Luca Nita, Chebona Bula, and four of their friends rode along the wagon train, taking in the strange sights. Chebona Bula asked, "Why they carry all those heavy things? Do not they have to go a long way?"

Luca Nita replied, "I have wondered the same thing; I don't know." They questioned many of the other peculiar travel practices, but Luca Nita had not asked why.

The Choctaw natives were still following when it was stopping time for the train. They formed their protective circle and started campfires to prepare the supper meal.

Luca Nita gathered up his friends and said, "If you want to stay for food, we should help by gathering firewood." He led them toward a nearby dry riverbed where they bundled up driftwood to take back to the wagon train.

Luca Nita and Chebona Bula ate with Elizabeth and Bill. The rest of the young braves divided up with several other families. After the meal, the natives gathered back together.

Chebona Bula suggested that they play a game called Kabucha, which was a form of stickball. Short sticks had to be retrieved from the firewood supplies and small nets fastened on the ends. "I have the Towa," Chebona Bula declared.

Luca Nita explained the rules to the group of pioneer youths gathered to participate. "This is the Towa," he said, holding up the small, leather-covered ball. Players must carry the Towa in their

Kabucha sticks. We have set up goal posts at each end of the playing field. A score is made when a player strikes the goal post with the Towa in their Kabucha stick or when they throw the Towa and it strikes the post. The winner will be the first team to reach twenty goals. Does all understand and agree?"

Joseph Walker, who was familiar with the game, served as the referee. He started the game by tossing the Towa ball up into the air, and Luca Nita jumped high to capture it in his Kabucha stick. The other Choctaws started blocking their opponents from pursuing Luca Nita, who immediately sprinted toward the goal post and, dodging around opponents, flipped the Towa, so it struck the post with a whack. His teammates rewarded him with a cheer. The Choctaws' familiarity with the game, coupled with their athletic dexterity, proved more than a match for the pioneer lads.

The few times the pioneers managed to capture the Towa, they either dropped it as they ran down the field, or their shots at the goal went wide. Steward was playing, and he didn't like to lose. He noticed that Chebona Bula was the high scorer for the Choctaw team. The next time one of the other braves had the Towa, he sought out Chebona Bula. Making it look accidental, Steward hit him from behind. He landed hard on his leg. Steward apologized and helped Chebona Bula to his feet, but he was hiding a grin when the young native limped away.

Nighttime was coming fast; and although the score was eighteen to two in favor of the Choctaw team, they ended the competition there, with the pioneer boys vowing to do better next time after they had time to practice first.

###

Around the campfire that night, Bill asked Walker to tell them more of his adventures as a mountain man and scout. Walker was happy to oblige.

"What do you want to hear about?" he asked.

"What did you do in Missouri, where you lived for a while?" Elizabeth asked.

"The only significant thing I did in Missouri was in 1827. I was elected the first sheriff of Jackson County. I served two terms, but eventually, I left because of the low pay."

"Why didn't you stay in California and hunt for gold?" someone asked.

"I have no desire to hunt for gold. But the Spanish authorities offered me a fifty-square-mile tract of land if I agreed to stay on and bring in fifty families to settle in Monterey, a town on the coast. I refused the offer. This was back in February of 1834. Instead, I led a party headed back east. At the base of the Sierras, we turned south in search of an easier crossing than the one we used on the westward trip. We found it, and it was later named Walker Pass."

"Will we be using Walker Pass to get into California?" Susan asked.

"No, that route is too far north for this train. After we get to Santa Fe, we will head south to pick up the new route I just surveyed last year for the Butterfield Stage Company. They haven't started using it yet, but I believe it is a much better route because it's easier to travel."

"What about your adventures with fur trapping?" someone asked.

"In 1834, Astor sold his fur-trading business to Ramsey Crooks and used the money to buy land in New York. When he died a few years later, he left over twenty million dollars to his children. The American Fur Company ceased trading in 1847. However, when the fur trade dried up a while back, I switched to horse and mule trading trips. Then I started guiding wagon trains to California and explored the Mono Lake area."

"Where is Mono Lake?" someone asked.

"It is a beautiful lake on the eastern slopes of the Sierras just east of Yosemite.

"In 1835, I became brigade leader of the American Fur Company. In 1808, John Jacob Astor, a German, had established the American Fur Company. Astor continued trading under the American Fur Company in the Rocky Mountains. By purchasing rivals such as the Rocky Mountain Fur Company—owned by myself and some other mountain men, including Tom Fitzpatrick, David Jackson, and William Sublette—he obtained a virtual monopoly of the United States fur trade."

As the old mountain man continued to recount some of his adventures, the pioneers slowly began to drift away to their own wagons, until the man was left alone with his memories staring into the fire.

Bill remarked to Elizabeth as they returned to their camp for the night, "I'm glad the questions for Walker steered clear of his fights with natives because of Luca Nita and his friends."

Chapter Eleven

JASON THE MERCHANT

GRASS VALLEY GOLDFIELD, CALIFORNIA

SEPTEMBER 15, 1853

Jason was talking to Long John as they watched over the children playing in the front yard of their new, enlarged home. "I tried to pan for gold, and it just doesn't work with only one hand. I've decided to go ahead and buy the general store. I've made arrangements with Adam to help out when I need someone to lift heavy boxes and such."

"Are you gonna rename it Jason's General Store?"

"No, I'll keep the store's name as Roussiere's General Store. Everyone knows it by that name, anyway."

"Do you plan on living in half of the structure like Roussiere did up until now?"

"No, I have plans for the rest of the structure. I'll keep it vacant for future store expansion."

"What kind of expansion were you thinking of?"

"I would like to add a line of mining machinery. Things like the turbine engines."

"Don't they destroy nature when they're used?" Long John asked.

"No, water turbines are generally considered a clean power producer. They use water for their energy source, and the turbine causes essentially no change to the water because it is only used to turn the turbine. And they are designed to operate for decades with little or no maintenance. I don't think hard rock mines around here are safe enough for the miners. I would also like to offer engineered timbers for shoring up the mine tunnels to make them structurally safer."

"Those ideas sound great! I think you are doing the right thing buying the store. Even if you hadn't lost your arm, it'd be a good business deal. You will more than likely make a lot more money and make it a lot faster than panning for gold like you've been doing."

Jason was relieved that the decision was made and that Long John supported it.

Later, since Jason figured he was done retrieving the rest of the Swede's gold stashes from the trees about the Bloomfield Mine, he decided to play a trick on the dishonest miners. He replaced the pokes of gold nuggets with pokes with rocks. He invited Long John and a few of the other miners to join him in staking out the area where he'd found the real gold stashes.

It didn't take long until they witnessed Luke and Stephen sneaking among the trees. They saw them locate one of the hiding places in an oak tree. While they held one of the pokes, they jumped in glee. Then Luke opened the poke, and their glee turned to dismay. They started cursing and threw the stones down in disgust.

Jason and his friends came out and confronted the two would-be thieves. "You know, gold is usually found in streams and obtained by some hard work. It's not found by spying on people and stealing the fruits of their labors."

Jason knew the only way they could have known to look in the oak trees was by spying on him.

Luke and Stephen stomped off in disgust.

Long John shouted after them, "Good riddance to bad rubbish."

Mike, one of the other miners, said, "I've had about enough from those two. I'm reporting this to the sheriff."

The next day, Jason was coming out of the bank in Centerville where he had deposited more of his and the Swede's gold. He had opened two separate accounts, one for himself and the other for Greta and Sven. After using some of the gold for building materials to build the kids' new home, Jason had deposited the rest in the bank for them to save.

News had gotten around the miners about Jason's ideas for expanding the general store, and most of them approved of his plans. With business picking up so much, Jason was able to lower the prices on many of the basic items he stocked, like gold pans, picks, and shovels. This served to bring in even more revenue.

Stopping at the post office to mail a letter for one of the miners, he was surprised to receive a letter from Elizabeth.

Darling Jason,

> I hope this finds you well and that you are missing me half as much as I miss you. I have decided to quit my teaching position and come to California to join you. Bill is coming with me, and we are leaving St. Louis tomorrow on the John Riker wagon train.

Jason stopped and checked the date on the letter. It was June 22. *That means she could be halfway here by now.* He was elated as well as dismayed. He was excited to see Elizabeth soon. But he was apprehensive about how she would react to his missing arm.

He continued reading Elizabeth's letter. It ended with:

> I don't know how long it will take to get to California, but we have a good wagon and team, and Bill promises to be a good chaperone. You don't need to worry about us; we are under God's protection.

> All my love,
> Elizabeth

Jason had built a permanent play area for the kids in a corner of his new general store. He watched Greta and Sven playing.

He found he had to push his way through a crowd of miners to see the children. It was so rare to have children in the mining camp. They were proving to be another unexpected draw for Jason's business.

Sven said to Greta, "I'm tired of playing dolls. Could we look at that picture book again?"

"Fine, I'll go get it."

Jason noticed Greta mothered her little brother a lot more since their pappy died. It seems to have helped Sven come out of his shell. He talked more—to his sister and Jason, at least.

Later, Long John, who was like a grandpa to the children, came by and took them for a hike in the woods. He had no special training on how to help traumatized kids, but his natural, compassionate nature was just what the children needed.

They were walking through the oak trees along Wolf Creek, and he pointed out wildlife as they went along.

"See that gray squirrel shimmying up that tree with a big, ol' pinecone?"

Both kids laughed, and Greta exclaimed, "How can he carry that pinecone so easily? It's bigger than he is!"

Sven chimed in, "What does he want with a pinecone anyway?"

"He eats the pine nuts. Squirrels think they're might tasty." Long John looked at Sven and was surprised. This was one of the few times Sven has opened up and actually talked to someone other than his sister or Jason.

On a rainy afternoon, Chin Lee came by the store.

Jason asked him, "Why don't you mine that claim over on Coyote Hill anymore?"

"Me no have that claim no more."

"Why not? Wasn't it paying off?"

"Yes, it pay plenty. It pay so much, Luke decided he wanted it and took it."

"That's not right. Can't you go to the sheriff about that?"

"I go to the sheriff. He say Chinaman had no rights for gold claim. And with the foreign miner's tax your government set, it cost more to mine than I make."

"Is that true? Has that happened to other Chinese in the goldfield?"

"Yes, it happen to many Chinamen. I think it better if we just do business like me with my laundry or Chow Long with his store that sells to other Chinamen. White men no want to wash clothes or eat China food, so they no bother us."

"Well, that foreign miners tax sounds completely unfair to me. I would not be surprised to see it repealed soon."

Jason was talking to some of the miners around the campfire one night. They were discussing the situation about Luke and Stephen.

"When I talked to the sheriff about those two scalawags, he said there was nothing he could do, since they didn't actually steal any of the Swede's gold," said Mike.

"That may be true, but we all know they tried their hardest. They should be held accountable for that, shouldn't they?" Long John asked.

Jason added, "What about all the other things they've done?"

"I didn't mention those to the sheriff."

"Someone should!" insisted Long John.

"There's always the miners' court," suggested Mike.

A miners' court was an informal group of miners who took it upon themselves to enforce law and order when the duly elected legal system failed or wasn't available.

"We'll just have to keep an eye on them as long as they stick around," Jason asserted.

In a way, he felt sorry for the two misfits, but he was tired of the trouble they'd caused in the goldfield. Secretly, he hoped they'd find some excuse to leave and take their troublesome antics with them for others to deal with.

Chapter Twelve

THE CAVALRY TO THE RESCUE

Approaching the New Mexico Badlands

September 15, 1853

Esther rode in the Dedmond wagon, which was being driven by Elizabeth. They were passing through an area that had marshland with tule bushes growing about shrinking ponds of water. The right, front wheel of their wagon squeaked in protest from not being greased lately.

After the death of her father, Esther had suffered a setback of sorts. She had withdrawn into her shell and avoided contact or communication with outsiders. She only spoke to Elizabeth and Bill.

"When are you going to be all better?" asked Esther.

"Soon, sweetheart. I'm feeling better every day."

"Will I get to go all the way to California with you?"

"You'll have to. She is joining her fiancé there," answered Bill, who was riding alongside the wagon.

"What is a fiancé? Will Bill be our new papa?" Esther asked.

Elizabeth corrected her. "No, Silly, Bill is my brother. He's sweet on Susan, anyway. And a fiancé is someone you intend to marry."

Esther retreated into her silence. In her mind, she had created an imaginary friend, Buster. *You're big and strong, Buster, and can take care of me.*

In camp one night, Dr. Freeman was conducting a follow-up examination with Elizabeth in her wagon. After doing so well in her recovery, she had suffered another relapse. "How are your symptoms? Is the pain in your abdomen doing better?" he asked her.

"It still hurts off and on."

"Have you had your women's time of the month since the accident?"

Elizabeth blushed in embarrassment but managed to shake her head no.

"Well, that doesn't bode well for having children in the future."

After the doctor left, Elizabeth very depressed. *What will Jason think of a new wife who can't have children? What will happen to our plans for a big family now?*

Sometime later, Elizabeth was driving her wagon while Esther sat inside the wagon. Bill came ridding up on Spot.

"How are you doing, Sis?"

"I'm doing all right. This was a good idea of yours for me to drive the wagon, even if it was so you would be free to scout with your friend, Walker," Elizabeth responded.

"Now, don't overtask yourself. You're still recovering. I'll be back later to check up on you." *I know she's still grieving the loss of Bob Sterling. I wonder, was it because she liked him more than she let on, or was it because his death was while he was trying to save her?* Bill rode away contemplating the answers to his unspoken questions.

"Esther, come sit closer to me," Elizabeth said.

Esther inched a little closer to Elizabeth.

Elizabeth hadn't talked to anyone, even her brother, about what Dr. Freeman had told her.

She regretted not being able to talk to someone about not having children. She decided to try and find out how Esther really felt. "Come sit up here on the seat next to me."

Esther reluctantly crawled up front and took a seat next to Elizabeth.

"How would you like it if you went to live with one of the other families, for instance Kimberly Thompson? She has those two little girls your age you play with."

Esther thought for only a moment before answering, "No! I want to live with you."

Elizabeth let out a breath she had been holding and gathered the little girl to her in a hug.

###

Walker and Luca Nita were on a scouting trip well ahead of the wagon train. Walker pulled his horse to a halt on a promontory overlooking a barren canyon. There wasn't a growing thing in sight, except for one lonely green tree growing on the desolate hillside.

"What could possibly cause that?" Walker was testing his new scout.

Luca Nita had not been through this part of the country before, but he knew what could cause the tree to grow. "There must be water come up from earth."

Walker complimented the brave and nodded in approval. "You're right. There's an underground stream that surfaces there. That's something we can use. We need to know every watering hole along the way."

They made their way toward the patch of green, and when they finally picked a trail through all the rocks and shale, they found a small pool of water. They both filled their water bottles and drank their fill of the refreshing water before letting their mounts do the same.

Elizabeth's thoughts centered around Bob Sterling and how he'd died trying to save her. As they crossed the dry, barren land, the dust and heat seemed to smother her like a blanket. But at least it brought her thoughts back to the present.

Elizabeth had finally been able to ride her new mount, while Bill drove their wagon alongside her. "I'm sure glad we added that extra water barrel to our wagon in El Paso. Some of the water holes that Scout Walker was counting on to supply the wagon train were dry."

Bill replied, "I never imagined that there was so much desert, rocks, and sand." The pioneers were rationing the water so only the people got to drink and even then, sparingly. The animals got to drink only when Walker could find a large enough water hole.

Walker came back from his latest scouting trip and stopped to tell Bill first. "Duffy Washington helped me and Luca Nita find a water hole that could be big enough to water all the stock. But we'll have to dig it out some first. Grab a couple of shovels and give us a hand."

He continued on and reported to Riker. Then snagging two fresh horses from the train's herd, he returned to Bill.

Following Walker's lead, Bill finally made his way over a low hill and down a grade to a sinkhole, where there was a puddle of foul-smelling water about ten feet across. Duffy was there with his witching stick. Luca Nita was digging already with a larger stick he'd found. Duffy had turned out to be a real asset to the wagon train because he had a knack for finding water.

Bill looked at it dubiously, and Walker said, "It will do for the stock but not for human drinking."

The four of them dug for quite some time until the water hole finally increased in size from a small pond to a medium lake. They continued digging, now standing in the water up to the middle of their boots. Finally, Walker said, "That's good. It will fill up on its own now."

It was almost dusk and time to stop for the night by the time the wagon train got to the water hole, so they circled up the wagons with the new water hole in the middle, so the stock could drink their fill throughout the night.

Around the campfire that night, Elizabeth spoke to John Riker. He once again reassured her, "We're on the right trail, and soon, we will cross the border into the New Mexico Territory."

Elizabeth asked, "How much more of this barren land do we have to go through before we reach California?" She motioned to the rocky land about them. There was not a tree or a blade of grass in sight.

Joseph Walker, who was throwing more buffalo chips on the fire answered, "It's pretty much like this the rest of the way. There are a few better areas we will pass through, but that isn't until after we cross over the Colorado River and get into California. The area about Bernardino is nice."

I hope we make it, thought Bill.

A few days later, Walker came galloping back to the train from a scouting trip. "Circle up," he ordered. "Luca Nita says there's a band of Ute natives headed our way, and they don't look friendly." Luca Nita had decided to go all the way to California and had been helping Walker scout for the wagon train.

Walker grabbed the team of the lead wagon and turned them to begin forming the circle. The rest of the wagons followed along, but they'd only formed about half of their protective circle when they were surrounded by hostile Ute natives.

Elizabeth and Bill placed her in their wagon and instructed Esther to stay down, so she would be safe.

The Ute attacked, riding around the partially circled wagons and shooting arrows as they rode. Bill lay prone under their wagon, shooting between the wheel spokes.

Elizabeth was busy at first reloading rifles, but it didn't take long before they were running low on ammunition.

Another wave of the attackers was repulsed by the pioneers with their superior weapons. The Utes only had a few rifles. Bill counted the balls and powder left for them to use in their defense. There weren't very many, and he regretted his failure to buy more when they were in El Paso. *We'll never last in a long, drawn-out battle,* he thought to himself.

Elizabeth soon found herself bandaging the wounded. There were getting to be too many for her and old Dr. Freeman to handle by themselves. She enlisted Susan to help her and the doctor. Susan about had a heart attack when one of the wounded turned out to be her father.

"Father, where are you hurt?"

"It's only a minor one, made with an arrow here in my left arm."

Bill loaded his last rifle. Suddenly, a bugle sounded, and blue-clad riders charged the surrounding braves. The Utes scattered and abandoned their attack on the wagon train. Bill and Elizabeth hugged each other in relief at their unexpected rescue. There had been about a dozen injuries, all non-life-threatening.

At the campfire later that night, Elizabeth sought out their rescuer, the U.S. cavalry captain. She stood in line to express her appreciation. Many of the train members did the same. He informed them that he was scouting for a possible route for a railroad all the way to the Pacific Coast. He agreed to accompany them as far as the Colorado River, ensuring the train's safety from any more hostile native attacks.

In four more days, they encountered the biggest river since the Arkansas. "This is the Colorado River," Walker informed them. "Everyone who's been having trouble with their wagon wheel rims getting loose, be sure and soak them overnight in the river, so the wood swells up tight again."

They all filled up their barrels with water in preparation for crossing the Mojave Desert on the other side of the Colorado.

Elizabeth asked, "Since we, and most everyone else, are getting short on salt, will we be able to store up more at the Salton Sea?"

Walker answered, "No, that salt is too contaminated, but I know of a salt cave you can get pure salt for cooking." Before leaving the next morning, Walker led those who needed it to the salt cave, and they chipped off enough salt to be ground down finer to restock their depleted supplies. They all marveled at the salt pillars rising from the cave's floor and extending to the low ceiling.

The next morning, Elizabeth sat on the seat of her wagon with the reins in her hands, as the wide expanse of the Colorado River stretched out before her. Bill was helping Susan and her family with the crossing, due to her father's injury in the Ute attack. A momentary regret flashed through Elizabeth's mind that Bob Sterling was not there to assist her as he had with the Arkansas River crossing. *I can do this*, she thought to herself. I've driven across several rivers on this journey west, although none as large as the Colorado.

Walker rode up beside her wagon, and seeing her anxiety, he tried to reassure her. "You can do this, Elizabeth. I will be here to help you and anyone else if they get into trouble."

It was her turn to start. Not wanting to hold up the crossing, Elizabeth cracked her whip, and the oxen stepped into the cold, swirling waters.

Walker kept pace with her and kept talking, more to reassure Elizabeth than anything else. "I scouted this crossing out good. It's all gently sloping shale along this stretch of the river. It's not like the limestone and sandstone further south of here that is easily eroded by the river. If you stay in line with the wagon ahead of you, you won't be in water higher than your wagon wheels. Just remember to keep the team moving; and if anything happens, which it won't, stay in the wagon."

The oxen didn't seem to be aware of Elizabeth's nervousness. They took it one step at a time. Reassured by their calmness and Walker's words, she relaxed somewhat. Then disaster struck. The right, front wheel had found a hole. The front of her wagon dropped sharply into the river, tipping her wagon hard to the right. The cargo not tied down in the wagon spilled out into the river and floated downstream. Wooden buckets and barrels bobbed in the swiftly moving current.

Walker immediately spurred his horse to the rescue. Elizabeth screamed in fright when the wagon tipped precariously but managed to retain her seat by dropping the reins and grabbing hold of the wagon seat. When Walker grabbed the harness of the stalled team and got it moving again, she breathed a silent prayer of thanks. *Thank You, Lord. Now just get me back on dry land.*

Neither the front wheels nor axle had been damaged. Walker guided the team the rest of the way across and yelled instructions to outriders on horses to grab the spilled cargo. They delivered most of it safely to dry land on the other side of the river.

Elizabeth breathed another prayer of relief when the oxen finally pulled her and her wagon safely onto the western shore of the Colorado River. Bill came over shortly after the incident, feeling guilty for not being there, and asked his sister, "What did we lose?"

"Just some food supplies, a harness for our spare ox, and some of your clothes."

"Well, I'll just have to do more hunting for food, and Luca Nita can show me how to make clothes like his."

###

The next morning, Bill and Susan walked alongside the wagons, to avoid eating the dust from the wagons being pulled by plodding oxen and horses.

"Are we really in California now?" said Susan. "It doesn't look like the 'land of milk and honey.'"

A little later, she had changed her mind and asked, "Isn't the dried-up salt lake beautiful?"

Bill agreed. "Yes, the crystals formed by the dried salt sparkle like diamonds. I wish they were diamonds, so I could use some for a ring for you."

"Why, Bill Dedmore, are you proposing to me?" She looked up at Bill and batted her beautiful, blue eyes.

"When I propose, you will know it for sure."

Susan remained silent as they continued their trek along the Southern Overland Trail, heartened by Bill's words: "When I propose . . ."

The two young pioneers joined hands and pulled up their bandanas to keep out the trail dust.

Meanwhile, Steward scowled as he viewed the closeness of the girl of his fancy and Bill.

Chapter Thirteen

CLAIM JUMPERS, BANDITOS, AND HORSE THIEVES

Grass Valley Goldfield, California

September 20, 1853

J ason got some interesting customers at the general store. One brisk, September morning, a beautiful Mexican lady came in looking for sewing supplies.

"Good morning. What can I help you with?" Jason asked.

"Buenos dias, señor. I am looking for thread to match the color of this chal." She fingered the crocheted shawl around her neck.

"I believe I can help you with that; come this way, señora. Or is it señorita?"

"I'm Señora Carmen Knight. And are you Monsieur Roussiere?"

"No, I am Jason Miller, the new proprietor of this fine establishment." Jason led his customer to the sewing section. Jason was a very patriotic citizen, and he had the California state flag displayed over the sewing section.

Upon seeing the flag, Señora Carmen commented, "That flag brings back memories."

"Oh, and what memories might that be?"

"Some years ago, I was crossing the Sacramento River on my late husband's ferry. My husband at that time was Dr. William Knight. I encountered a man who happened to be the secretary for Governor Castro of the Mexican state of California. We struck up a conversation, and he inadvertently revealed to me secret plans for the delivery of a herd of horses needed to enforce a recent decree to the effect that no non-Mexicans could own land and must leave California.

"Well, I informed my husband, and he left the next morning to warn Captain Fremont of these plans. Fremont encouraged a group of private patriots to act, which they did. They succeeded in diverting these horses from reaching Castro's forces in Santa Clara and delivered them instead to Fremont. These patriots, under the belief that they had started a revolution, then rode to Sonoma and captured General Marion Vallejo. They couldn't have the Mexican flag flying over the now-American town. They believed all good revolutions deserved their own flag, so they designed this new flag of the Republic of California. Believe it or not, the animal on the flag is supposed to be a bear—even though it more closely resembles a hog—hence the name of the Bear Flag Revolt."

"That is a very interesting story, Señora Carmen, and one my fiancée would enjoy very much."

"I would love to meet your fiancée."

"If you return in a few weeks, you may do just that. Unfortunately, she is still on her way here from Iowa."

Señora Carmen was leaving with her purchase when she passed by the bulletin board near the entrance. She stopped abruptly and stared at a wanted poster that hung there. It was the poster for Joaquin Murrieta.

"This cannot be. This is my cousin Joaquin. I have known him since he was a niño. There must be some mistake."

"You are related to the notorious bandito Joaquin Murrieta, who has been terrorizing the gold country?"

"Si, señor. It would seem so. But I have been away for some time. I heard his wife and brother had been killed but nothing of him becoming a bandito. This is most disturbing."

Jason was a little disturbed to have a relative of Murrieta's in his store. Nevertheless, he wanted to reassure the lady. "I am sure there is some mistake. No one related to a lady of your refinement could possibly be a bandito."

The next day when Mr. Roberts strode into Jason's general store, Jason, who had been dusting a shelf of canned goods, asked him about the children's book *Der Struwwelpeter*.

Mr. Roberts said, "*Wissen Sie, es istschonseltsam.* There's a funny thing about that book. Heinrich Hoffmann wrote and drew pictures for the book in 1845 when he could not find any suitable children's books. It was for his son, and each chapter is a story telling why children shouldn't be bad."

Jason smiled and said, "My kids are well-behaved, so I guess the fact that they can't read German doesn't really matter much. By the way, what does *Der Struwwelpeter* translate to?"

"It means 'Slovenly Peter.' That's the title of the first story in the book."

Jason asked, "He couldn't come up with a better title, huh? Sometime, when you are free, could you translate some of the stories for my children?"

"I'd be happy to," Mr. Roberts replied. "It is considered the very first child picture book published in the whole world." He then went about collecting the items he needed.

As Jason returned to his dusting, he glanced at the children in his care. As summer was drawing to a close, the kids spent most of their daytime in the play area of the general store Jason had set aside for them. They liked to play with their toys—Sven with his building blocks and Greta with her dolls.

He reflected on how the children had recovered from their father's death in the mine cave-in, each in their own way.

Since Jason had recovered from his own accident enough to take over supervising them full time, Sven had opened up to him somewhat. He found that when he spent more undivided time with Sven, the boy responded better—with him, at least. He now answered Jason's direct questions, but not much else. He didn't interact with other kids well, not that there were many in the gold camp. This still worried Jason.

Greta, on the other hand, showed that she had adjusted better to the situation. She mothered her little brother and tried to get him to interact with her and their pets. She picked up the gray kitten that had attached itself to Sven and placed it in his lap.

Mr. Roberts leaned over the counter with the purchases he collected and asked Jason, "I hear they start school in Grass Valley? Are you planning on putting the children in it when it starts up again?

Jason stroked his wooden hand and replied, "Yes, I do plan to do that. I just hope Sven will be well enough by then to do okay. I worry that he still won't be interacting with other children, by then."

"Is the child not well?"

"He misses his mother and father still."

Mr. Roberts stood up from leaning on the counter and, walking over to a display of shovels, changed the subject. "The thing really on mind is my stream, where I'm working my claim, is going away. It's making it hard to work."

"That's strange. Why are you worried? I would think that would make it easier to get at the gold. You don't have to wade about in all that cold water. What stream are you panning, anyway?"

Mr. Roberts replied, "I'm working on Cherry Creek."

"Well, it's that time of the year when most of the small streams dry up. What are you planning to do this winter if we don't get any rain and you still can't pan for gold?"

"I was worried about that, too."

"Well, if that happens, check back with me. I may have something for you to do around the store."

"Thank you, thank you, I appreciate that very much!"

After Mr. Roberts left with his purchases, Jason was worrying as he stocked shelves at his store when Long John came in. Jason said, "I'm really getting concerned about Elizabeth. I know it sometimes takes six months for the trip from St. Louis to California by wagon train, and it has only been a little over three months, but I'm imagining all kinds of bad things happening. If Elizabeth and Bill are taking the northern route, like I did when I came to California, they could almost be to the Sierras by now."

Long John interjected, "I've not heard of any snow yet up there in the Sierras, but I've heard of snow during July before, so you can never tell."

Jason continued, "If they are taking the southern route, they could be lost in the desert somewhere. All I can think to do is pray and leave their fate in the Lord's hands." He was glad that he could at least do that now. It was some improvement over the disconnection he had felt between himself and God because of his accident.

"Well, my boy, you did get that letter from Elizabeth. She seems the sort to get you news if anything bad happened. I wouldn't worry too much."

A few days later, Jim Buchanan walked into the general store and posted another notice on the bulletin board about jobs open for Mr. McKnight of the Gold Hill Mine. Somehow, the first one disappeared. Jason read it and felt like tearing it up and throwing it away as well. Before he had a chance, some of the miners hanging around the store noticed it and started discussing the subject.

"I still say those hard rock mines are way too dangerous unless the owner is willing to spend what it takes to make them safe for the workers. I don't trust McKnight to do that at his Gold Hill Mine," Mike said.

"But I've been down in that mine, and I say it's safe," Stephen claimed.

"If you think it's so safe, why aren't you working there?" asked Long John.

"I have other plans," Stephen muttered low.

Jason spoke up. "I'm surprised you two are still here. There are other alternatives, you know, rather than going to work for McKnight."

"What might those be, then?" asked Luke.

"We could form one of those cooperative groups like they have over in Nevada City. A group that works together to dam up a stream, so it's rerouted, and that makes it easier to get at the gold that way," Jason suggested. "But you have to be careful how you build the dam. You have to leave enough water running, so you can use it to wash away the silt and gravel."

"That's a right good point," Long John agreed. "Kenneth, you've had more book learning than the rest of us. Could you draw up some kind of agreement and make it all legal like?"

There were shouts of agreement from the rest of the miners assembled. Jason was glad they were taking his suggestion seriously.

Luke and Stephen faded away from the back of the group. And once outside and out of hearing, Luke said, "How are we going to ever start collecting those fees if we don't have anyone willing to go over and work for McKnight?"

"And that's only if they sign up in a week's time, which is almost up," added Stephen.

"We're going to have to do something more drastic to make this deal work," Luke said.

"That's right. But I've got an idea. Come on. Let's go."

Jason's claim on Wolf Creek was being worked by a Nisenan native he'd hired. He was doing well until Luke and Stephen came by and started taking advantage of him.

"Where are your papers, Redskin?" Luke demanded.

"My paper is in bag on horse."

Stephen came up, leading the native's horse. "You mean, this horse that was reported stolen last week?"

The native knew he'd caught and broken that horse himself. But he also knew the penalty for horse stealing and did not want to take any chances with Luke and Stephen, who had bad reputations. He turned and, without another word, walked away.

But Luke noticed the Nisenan had the gold he had accumulated in a poke on his belt. He started to object. "Now wait a minute, Redskin—"

Stephen interrupted, "Let him go. Now, we have the claim and a new horse to boot."

The Nisenan took the gold to Jason at the general store and told him about the claim jumpers.

"Are those scoundrels still pulling their shenanigans? Don't worry, I'll take care of it, and I'll see about getting your horse back, too."

###

Long John stood up, stretching his arms over his head to get a kink out of his back. A group of about ten miners had just finished a crude log and rock dam across Wolf Creek. The weather was cool with some clouds covering the sun. "This should help a lot in the panning for gold from now on," he said.

"How do we keep other miners from coming in and taking advantage of our hard work?" Joseph asked.

"That's why we worked so hard to get everyone downstream from this dam to sign up and join in this group," Long John said.

Wolf Creek was still running but just strong enough to be useful to the miners when separating the gravel from the gold.

It was getting on to dark, and the miners trooped off to their respective camp sites or shacks for the night.

Watching the activity in Wolf Creek from bushes along the bank where they were well-hidden, Luke nudged Stephen. "Let's give them a while, and then we can get to work busting this dam."

"But they'll know something is wrong when they see the stream flowing strong again," Stephen said.

"You're right. I guess we'll just have to get up early before dawn and do it then," Luke replied.

###

Later that evening, Jason and his native friend went looking for Luke and Stephen. Jason wanted to confront them about jumping his claim on Wolf Creek. Jason shook the papers in their faces and heatedly declared, "This is my claim, as you two very well know. I had my friend here working it, and he has papers showing that, if you had bothered to look at them."

Luke replied in a weaseling voice, "How were we supposed to know? You can't expect us to keep track of where every miner's claim is!"

Jason continued, "And furthermore, that horse you took had a Nisenan brandmark on the horse's left shoulder. See there?" He showed them the horse's left shoulder.

"So, what are you going to do about it, Crip?" Luck snarled.

Jason was unarmed, but the native was ready. Jason turned toward him, and he tossed a shotgun to Jason, who caught it with his good hand and leveled it at Luke and Stephen.

The two would-be claim jumpers and horse thieves almost stumbled over each other in their haste to run away.

"Thanks for covering for me with those two," Jason said. They returned to their homes for the evening, Jason to the newly renovated Swede's house to relieve Long John, who was caring for the kids, and the native to Jason's old shanty, which he now occupied.

When the miners showed up at Wolf Creek the next morning, it was flowing strong, like it had before. Logs and rocks were scattered along the banks.

Long John swore under his breath. "Now we have to build that dam all over again."

"I got better things to do than build that dam all over again," said Walter.

"Who do you think did it?" asked Joseph.

"I'll bet my last dollar, it was those two no-goods, Luke and Stephen. We should have run them out of Grass Valley when we caught them trying to steal the Swede's gold." Long John puzzled over the dilemma but finally said, "I know. When we get the dam rebuilt, we'll stand guard and catch them in the act."

Early the next morning, Long John and some of the other miners were hidden in the brush guarding the dam across Wolf Creek that they had rebuilt. Luke and Stephen were seen attacking the structure again. They started throwing the rocks and logs up on the banks. The miners jumped out and grabbed the two scoundrels. They dragged them down to where many miners were congregated before scattering to work their claims.

"We've caught Luke and Stephen red-handed trying to destroy the dam on Wolf Creek for the second time. What shall we do with these fellows?" Long John asked the mob of angry miners.

"String 'em up!"

"Tar and feather 'em!"

"Run 'em out on a rail!"

These were just some of the suggestions coming from the angry mob.

"Has anyone got a rail handy?" Long John shouted.

Someone produced two fence posts, and Long John said, "These will do."

The unlucky pair was quickly tied up and mounted on the posts and borne out of Boston Ravine.

"You can't do this," pleaded Stephen, as he squirmed to free his hands.

Luke joined in with, "We didn't do nothing; let us go."

Their whining and excuses turned to screams of pain when the hot tar was brought out and poured over their bodies. The feathers came next, and the miners' court bore the two claim jumpers out of Boston Ravine and deposited them, still screaming, on the bank of Wolf Creek. The two soon found that jumping into the creek was little help in relieving their pain and getting rid of the tar and feathers.

After several hours of excruciating pain, Stephen finished removing the last of the tar from Luke's back.

"Ouch! Take it easy, can't ya?"

"You're such a wimp! You weren't exactly gentle with my back."

"What are we gonna do now? Where do we go from here?"

"I heard they're finding color in Bear River down south. I think we've worn out our welcome in these parts."

Jason had many worries. At night, he often tossed and turned as his worries kept him awake. He was worried—not only about claim jumpers, but also about how Elizabeth was doing on her journey west. When Jason was worried, he had a place he liked to go to. It was a shady oak grove at the bottom of a hill on Rattlesnake Creek. Despite the name, it was a place where he felt closest to God. It was located about halfway between Grass Valley and Auburn, just off the Emigrant Trail.

He often went there to renew his spirit. He stopped in a glen halfway up the hill to the ridge and listened to the sounds of nature— the birds chirping the faint hum of insects and the tinkle of the water leaping from ledge to ledge. Today, there was a gentle breeze that stirred the leaves in the trees, making the blossoming flowers nod as if in agreement that all was right in the world. All these things worked to calm Jason's soul and soothe his spirit. He felt a connection to God once again. He realized Long John had been right. God hadn't abandoned him. He had lost contact with God for a time because of his own efforts—or lack of effort—to stay connected. He had recovered from his accident and could now use his left hand as well as he had his right. He wasn't stuck in a cold stream panning for grains of gold anymore. He vowed, then and there, to keep this new closeness with God, no matter what it took.

Jason was working in his store late one night just before closing when several of the miners came in for supplies. They were hard rock miners and knew Jason had been one of the independent miners. They deliberately asked to see some heavy equipment that was up on a high shelf. They stood around waiting to see what Jason would do. He simply pulled out a contraption he had engineered and built from the back room. It was a platform that worked by a pulley system. He maneuvered it into position and raised it to the high shelf's level. Then he mounted a ladder placed beside his contraption and maneuvered the piece of equipment onto the platform with his good hand.

He then descended the ladder and lowered the platform to the ground level. The miners just stood there with their mouths hanging open in wonderment. They'd come in to harass Jason, but instead, they'd been impressed by his ingenuity. With his new invention, Jason had not had to call on Adam to help him after all.

The hard rock miners were so impressed, they stayed for Jason's demonstration of the piece of equipment.

"That's gotta save us a lot of work," declared their leader. "I'm going to tell McKnight about this here contraption."

Jason was tidying up the broom display in his store when several rough-looking strangers entered. As they strode by the bulletin board, which was near the store's entrance, one of the men stopped and pointed out one of the wanted posters posted there. All the men laughed as their leader snatched the poster off the board and tore it up, discarding the pieces on the floor. The poster was the one for Joaquin Murrieta, the notorious Mexican bandit known all over the gold country as the Robin Hood of El Dorado.

"You won't need that anymore," the leader announced in a loud, bragging voice.

"Why's that?" Jason asked, as he picked up the pieces of the poster.

"Because as duly appointed members of the California Rangers, we just apprehended and killed Murrieta and his gang. We caught them over by Coalinga trying to rob a stagecoach. In the shootout, I plugged Murrieta, and Monte here got Manuel Garcia, better known as 'Three-fingered Jack.'"

"Did you keep any proof?" someone asked.

"We sure did. We took Murrieta's head and Garcia's hand. They were good enough to get us the governor's reward of one thousand dollars each."

This announcement caused a big stir with the miners gathered in Jason's store. Most of the miners were happy that such a notorious bandit had been eliminated. But some were more sympathetic with Murrieta, who reportedly had been discriminated against just because he was Mexican. He and his brother had been accused of horse theft, his brother hung, and Joaquin's wife raped and murdered. They saw him as a hero because he had distributed much of the stolen gold to needy miners.

Later that very week, Jason was on his way to Nevada City to make a Wells Fargo deposit. He carried two bulging saddlebags full of gold nuggets and gold dust. He was riding a horse of his own he had recently acquired. He was armed with both a shotgun on a sling over his shoulder and a pistol in a left-handed holster.

He came through the oak woodland on a well-used trail when suddenly, a band of highwaymen burst out of the brush with drawn pistols. "Esta atraco, señor—your gold or your life."

Caught by surprise, Jason didn't resist and raised his hands in surrender. He handed over the saddlebags filled with gold. His biggest regret was that the last of the Swede's gold was included with the rest of the gold he was carrying.

The gang leader was fastening the gold onto his horse when one of his men rode forward and said, "I know you, señor. Do you not work for Roussiere? Are you not the hombre who lost his arm trying to save the Swede in the mine cave-in?"

Jason just held up his fake wooden arm in reply.

"Joaquin, this is the hombre that was the Swede's amigo and is taking care of his niños."

Jason stiffened in his saddle in surprise. He didn't bother correcting the bandit about him now owning the general store. Could this really be the notorious Joaquin Murrieta, whom some claimed robbed from the rich only to give to the poor and was supposed to be dead?

The bandito stepped forward and returned the saddlebags to Jason, saying, "Perdóname, señor. Put these to good use, por favor."

Jason replied, "Part of this is going to finish building a new home for the Swede's orphans."

"Bueno, that's muy bueno."

"Are you really Joaquin Murrieta?"

"Si, señor. The rumors of my demise are just that—rumors."

"But the posse came into the store and said they had proof that it was you they captured and killed."

"Must I remind you, señor, that there are several banditos named Joaquin roaming these hills, and the rangers and I have never met face to face."

With that, the bandito whipped off the mask that had covered his face, and Jason recognized him from his wanted poster. It was, indeed, Joaquin Murrieta.

As Jason continued on his way, he was still shaking his head in bewilderment. As he delivered the gold to the Wells Fargo office, he wondered how the California Rangers had gotten their rewards with the head and hand of the wrong banditos.

Jason thought, *I've got some reassuring news for one pretty señora when she comes into my store next time.*

Chapter Fourteen

A NEW FAMILY IS FORMED

Mojave Desert

September 20, 1853

While Bill scouted with Walker, Steward pressed his luck with Susan. He saw no other way to win Susan, other than by undermining her obvious growing affection for Bill.

"When we get to California, what is the first thing that you want to do?" Steward asked her.

"I'm going to settle down and start a big family. How about you?"

"I'm going to get me some of those peaches that grow as big as watermelons and have my mother make me a giant cobbler. I love peach cobbler."

"Do you really think they grow that big in California?"

Steward was a practical guy, but he didn't mind embellishing something for effect. "Sure, they do; otherwise all of this rotten trip would have been for nothing."

"Yeah, there is that." Susan laughed. "Have you ever talked to someone who has actually been to California?"

"Other than Joseph Walker and John Riker, no. You are getting mighty close to Bill. I sure hope nothing happens to him when he's out scouting for the wagon train with Walker."

"Bill can take care of himself," Susan asserted.

Steward tried another tack. "Bill sure is set on striking it rich in California. He's got the gold fever bad. Won't you prefer someone who is willing to settle down and start a family?"

This got Susan comparing Steward with Bill in her mind. *Steward, you are very funny, clever with words, good-looking with your dark hair and brooding eyes . . . But there's something about you, Mister. Something just doesn't ring true about you. I can see myself settling down and raising a family with Bill, even if he doesn't strike it rich in the California goldfield. He may have the Sierra gold fever, but there's more to him than that.*

Luca Nita was standing guard duty along with Bill when Steward approached Bill. "There were three horses stolen from the remuda last night, and you still are friends with that redskin. When are you going to get wise to the fact that he probably arranged for them to go missing?"

Bill replied, "I don't believe Luca Nita had anything to do with it."

"I'm taking my suspicions to Riker. We'll see what he has to say."

The next morning Riker, along with Steward and an angry group of around twenty men, confronted Luca Nita along with Bill and Elizabeth at their wagon.

A large blacksmith named Oren took control, stating, "We think this redskin had something to do with our missing stock. What do you have to say about it?"

Bill intervened for his friend. "Wait a minute here. Luca Nita wasn't even on duty that night. How could he be involved?"

"Where were you then?" Oren demanded.

"Me eat with Bill and Elizabeth, then sleep under wagon with Bill."

"That's right, and I'm a light sleeper. I would have known if he left," Bill verified.

"Sure, he's gonna stick up for his redskin friend," Steward said.

Elizabeth stepped in. "I can verify the supper part and that they went to bed under the wagon. I slept inside and could have heard anyone leaving or coming back during the night."

"So, you have an alibi. You still could have arranged things beforehand and not had to leave that night at all," asserted Oren.

Riker finally stepped in. "All right, that's enough. We have no proof that Luca Nita had anything to do with the theft. We don't believe for a minute that you had anything to do with the theft, Luca Nita. But if Luca Nita leaves and doesn't return to the wagon train, that will end the matter."

There were several of the group that voiced displeasure with the decision; but Riker's decision prevailed, and they continued getting ready to move out for the day.

Elizabeth and Bill assured Luca Nita, "We don't believe for a minute that you had anything to do with the theft."

Bill accompanied Luca Nita as he packed his horse and prepared to leave. "I'm sorry to see you go. I'll miss you, my friend."

The weather was mighty hot for September. Oxen and horses were suffering, and Riker called a train-wide meeting one morning. He told everyone assembled, "I've decided we have to start traveling at night. Everyone should be rationing your water. We will rest up today and start out at dusk tonight."

Everyone was relieved by the extra day's rest but concerned for the reason. A lot of folks couldn't adjust so quickly, and not many got any extra sleep that day. Instead, they mostly sat about in little groups discussing their chances of making it out of the desert in one piece.

Susan and Bill found a secluded place where they could talk alone. Susan asked, "What do you really think of our chances?"

Bill replied, mostly to reassure Susan, "I trust Walker and Riker to get us through. They've done this before, and even though it's a new trail for them, others have made it." Noticing her still apprehensive look, he impulsively opened his arms. "Here, let me hold you for a bit."

Susan willingly welcomed his embrace and stood for a long while, relishing the feel of his strong arms about her, protecting her from her worries.

Bill's confidence grew as he realized how much Susan believed in him and his abilities. She depended on him, and he vowed to himself that he wouldn't let her down.

Their night treks were well-lit at first by a nearly full moon. The train spread out over the desert landscape so as few as possible had to eat their neighbor's dust. They passed by the Salton Sea, and few of the pioneers had to be cautioned to avoid it and keep their stock away as well. The skeletal remains of other animals who hadn't known the deadly consequences of drinking the salty water were enough to keep them clear.

Duffy Washington was having a hard time keeping up with the rest of the wagon train. The mules that pulled his decrepit, old wagon were just as old and tired. Finally, about a night's travel beyond the Salton Sea, Bertha dropped dead in her tracks. Bill, who was walking and leading his horse, Spot, stopped at Duffy's wagon to lend assistance.

"I's don't know what I's gonna do," exclaimed Duffy. "Poor old Bart can't haul us all by himself."

"Why don't I lend you my horse until you can find another mule to take Bertha's place?" Bill offered.

"I's can't take your bestus horse, Master Bill," Duffy protested.

"I don't need him right at the moment. Walker is scouting the trail now, anyway."

So, they hitched up Spot alongside Bart, and Duffy tried getting underway again. But Spot and Bart didn't get along all that well and weren't a very good team, so Bill went looking for another solution to Duffy's predicament.

Late the next day, before the wagon train got started for the night, Bill was on foot looking for firewood and came across a very strange sight just over the rise from where the wagons were camped. He found two very strange-looking animals. They were lying down when Bill first spotted them. As he got closer, they looked a little like cattle, except they had longer necks. As he got still closer, one of them stood up, and he saw that they had extremely long legs as well. When they turned to the side, he saw they also had a large hump on their backs.

"What in the world?" he muttered. "I believe they look like the camels I saw once in a book. But what are camels doing out here in the Mojave Desert?" They didn't shy away that much as he approached them. With Bill's way with animals, he soon had them on leads, fashioned from the rope he carried. "You guys must be used to humans handling you," he said. He continued talking to them in a soft, soothing voice as he led them back to the wagon train.

He created quite a stir as he arrived, and Duffy was the first to comment. "Goodness, Master Bill, what are dem creatures you got there?"

John Riker came forward and explained, "I heard a story about a guy named Beale who was in charge of an army experiment using camels out here in the desert, back before 1850. They were in Texas for a while; then they were moved to California. Some of them must have gotten loose out here, and these are the survivors."

"Well, however they got here, they might just be Duffy's answer to prayer. That is, if they can be harnessed and will pull his wagon," Walker exclaimed.

Many of the pioneers laughed at the idea, but Bart Smith, Susan's father, came forward, saying, "I'm a teamster, and I think I can rig up harnesses for these beasts so they can pull your wagon, Duffy. Let me give it a try."

The wagon train's departure that night was delayed slightly as Bart and Duffy fashioned harnesses and bridals for the two camels, which were a little reluctant as first. They didn't take to being harnessed side by side.

Finally, Bart declared, "We must lengthen the wagon's tongue shaft, and we just need to rig it for one camel. I think one will pull this wagon just fine." They managed to add on by splicing on enough length onto the shaft from some discarded wagon parts found along the trail. Finally, they had the biggest camel, which Susan had named Boomer, harnessed and ready to pull the wagon. They tied Marigold, the smaller female, on behind. The wagon train got underway, with Duffy's strange-looking wagon and team trailing behind.

A few weeks later, the wagon train reached Bernardino. Elizabeth was pleasantly surprised as the wagon train came out of the desert into this place of singular beauty. She immediately saw why the Spanish had established a settlement in Bernardino and called it the Place of Plenty. The dry desert ended and gave way to gardens. There must have been some kind of irrigation system because the gardens contained terrace after terrace of not only many vegetables and fruit trees but also a surprising variety of blooming flowers as well. As the wagon train made its way out of the desert, their vantage point was still high enough to give a sweeping view of the foothills that gradually leveled out into the valley below.

They camped the first night at the old Spanish mission. But instead of the Spanish padres, the Mormons were there to welcome the wayfarers from Riker's wagon train. The Mormons were very enterprising in their settlement of nearby Utah, Bernardino being on a natural supply route.

Bill questioned one of the Mormon leaders named John Billings about the history of the Spanish missions in California.

Billings told him, "The Spanish founded their missions in Alta California between 1769 and 1823. There were twenty-one missions in all, built primarily to establish Spain's claim of colonizing the West Coast of the new world. They stretched from San Diego to Sonoma, fifty miles north of San Francisco. In 1821, Mexico achieved independence from Spain, taking Alta California and the twenty-one missions along with it, but the missions continued to maintain authority over natives and control of land holdings until the 1830s. At the peak of its development in 1832, the coastal mission system controlled an area equal to approximately one-sixth of Alta California. The Alta California government secularized the missions after the passage of the Mexican Secularization Act of 1833. That marked the demise of most of the missions, including the one in Bernardino."

The wagon train spent several days in Bernardino recuperating from the ordeal of crossing the desert. Steward, not being easily discouraged, made one last attempt at winning Susan's hand because he had fallen in love with the country around Bernardino and wanted to settle there.

"Susan, I know you like this place. Stay here with me and settle down. We could have a good life here."

"You're right, Steward. I do love what I see here in Bernardino. But I'm afraid I don't love you. You see, I've fallen in love with Bill, and I'm following him to the goldfields up north."

Five days later, the wagon train arrived in Los Angeles. Bill was a little disappointed. It was nothing more than a village. He asked Walker, "Where is the glorious city of Los Angeles I've heard so much about?"

Walker informed him, "Los Angeles hasn't grown much in the past twenty years. It was built inland on the Río Porciúncula, rather than by the ocean. This was done because it would have been too exposed to attacks by enemies from the ocean. As you can see, it was constructed in the traditional Spanish style, centered about a rectangle consisting of a city plaza, a guardhouse, a townhouse, a granary, and of course, a mission."

A few days later, Bill and Susan were standing on a bluff overlooking the Pacific Ocean. This was the first time either of them had seen the Pacific Ocean—or any ocean, for that matter.

"What a beautiful sight!" exclaimed Bill. "Did you ever think there could be so much water in one place? Listen to the roar of the waves. It's almost sounds like God is breathing," Bill murmured.

"Smell the sea air—like the great salt flats, only wet."

They both watched the seagulls gliding on the wind currents and diving into the breaking waves for fish. The sun was setting, a great orange ball sinking into the ocean on the horizon, leaking orange, red, and yellow into the clouds near it and reflecting in the ocean waters. Peace filled the air there, where the land met the ocean. It made up for the hardships and the ordeals they had endured crossing the wilderness.

Bill held Susan's hand, and he turned to face her. Dropping to one knee, he stared speechless into his sweetheart's eyes.

"What are you doing, Bill?" Susan asked with a little laugh.

"I'm asking y-you . . . will you p-p-please be my wife?"

Realization dawned on Susan. "Yes, yes, a thousand times yes. I'll be your wife."

Bill shot to his feet, and Susan leapt into his arms. They sealed their engagement with a long, passionate kiss.

The wagon train arrived at the Mission Santa Ynéz a few days later. It was located thirty-five miles north of Santa Barbara. The mission sat in the fertile Santa Ynéz Valley amongst vineyards and orchards planted by the mission padres.

John Riker told them, "I like using the old Spanish missions as rest stops. Many of them are abandoned now by the church, but some are still active. This one was purchased by a private individual and is well-maintained."

At dinner that night, Susan noted the size of the peaches and remembered Steward's comment. Although not quite as big as watermelons, as Steward had imagined, they were impressively large. She asked Bill, "Have you ever seen peaches this big?" As she took a huge bite out of hers, the sweet juice dripped down and off her chin.

The members of the wagon train enjoyed the sumptuous fruits and vegetables grown in this rich, agricultural region.

###

When the wagon train traveled along the coast, Elizabeth asked John Riker, "Is this still called the Overland Trail?"

"No," Riker responded. "We are now on the El Camino Real. That is Spanish for the Royal Highway."

Later, as the wagon train traveled along the coast, they came to places where a ravine had cut into the shoreline, and they had to travel further inland to get around them.

Elizabeth remarked, "Don't you just love the views of the ocean with their sandy beaches? Look at the colors of the rocky shoreline cliffs—tan, brown, white, and red."

"I really like all the little islands offshore. I wish we had time to stop and explore some of them," Bill remarked.

"You can't even get down to the beach in most places," Esther commented.

"Typically, the coastal cliffs are so steep and rugged, they make it impossible to scale them to get down to the ocean," Elizabeth noted. "But in some places, the pine trees and shrubs grow on a gradual slope, and we could get down to the beaches."

###

Eventually, the travelers came to a giant forest that made Bill stop in his tracks, and he gaped in amazement.

"Those have to be the redwood trees Walker bragged about," Bill exclaimed to Susan.

"Wow, they could reach almost to Heaven," Susan responded.

The wagon train had arrived at the area known as Santa Cruz, just south of San Francisco. They camped at the old Spanish mission located there.

Susan asked the padre at the mission, "Do you know the history of this mission?"

Padre Sebastian informed the pioneers, "Santa Cruz was one of the original twenty-one counties named when California became a state in 1851. The mission at Santa Cruz was founded in 1791. There are many beautiful redwood trees located near us."

Later, as Bill and Susan strolled through the redwood forest, Bill said to Susan, "These magnificent trees make me feel almost holy, just walking through this silent forest."

"Even those that have fallen are taller than you could ever reach, Bill. I love the leafy, green ferns all along the winding paths. Look at this hollow, fallen tree; we could both easily fit inside." They stood holding hands, both feeling the reverent atmosphere that permeated the redwood forest.

"Do you think these trees were here when Christ walked on this earth?" Bill asked Susan.

"It makes my heart sing to think we can actually touch something that Christ could have touched—if He'd ever been in America."

Bill and Susan walked along the redwood aisles, both contemplating the passing of the ages. The calming silence seemed to engulf them in solitude as they admired God's handiwork.

"What do you say about us getting married right here, sweetheart?" Bill asked Susan.

"Oh, I love that idea, Bill, darling."

So, the next day, nearly the whole wagon train gathered in the redwood grove eagerly awaiting the wedding of Bill and Susan. They had enlisted the services of Padre Sebastian from the mission to perform the ceremony.

"One of you must be Catholic for me to perform this ceremony. Which one is it?"

"I am Catholic," Susan replied.

"Then you, young man, must agree to raise any children in the Catholic church. Do you agree?"

"I agree," Bill replied.

Susan's papa waited to walk her down the aisle, formed by fallen redwood trees, to give her away. "You look lovely, my dear. Your mother and I are so happy for you. We both agree that Bill is a fine man. He will make a good husband."

When Susan's mother and father learned about the couple's engagement, they'd bought a wedding gown for her in Santa Barbara with nearly the last of their money. The white Victorian gown had a high neck with Chantilly lace yoke; long sleeves; a cap overlay with an elaborate, heavily embellished lace bodice; a fitted waist; and a trumpet bottom. Her mother still had the veil she had been married in, one of the few items that had survived the trip unharmed. Susan wore it. She also presented her daughter with an ivory cross that Susan wore on a necklace. Elizabeth helped arrange Susan's hair. It was parted in the middle and pinned back with tiny braids, also fastened back. The veil covered her hair.

Susan clung to her father's arm as they walked down the aisle. When Bill first caught sight of his bride, he said a silent prayer. *Thank You, Lord, for such a lovely bride and for bringing us here safely. And please get us the rest of the way to the goldfield safely.*

Chapter Fifteen

IT ALL COMES TOGETHER

Grass Valley Goldfield, California

October 23, 1853

"Where are those kids of yours?" Mr. Roberts greeted Jason as he came into the store. "I have time to read some of those stories from *Der Struwwelpeter*. They are poetry really."

"Great! Let me get them. They are out back playing on the swing I made for them. It looks like a storm's brewing; I was going to call them in anyway."

He soon returned with both children.

"Yay, Mr. Roberts, we've been dying to hear the stories that go with the pictures in our book," Greta greeted him enthusiastically. She was dragging one of her dolls by one arm.

Sven hung back, not sure of this man he had met but barely knew.

Mr. Roberts sat down in one of the wooden chairs grouped about the potbellied stove in the back of the store. Greta handed him the book and stood beside the chair with Sven behind her, peeking around his big sister's shoulder.

"What does *Der Struwwelpeter* mean, Mr. Roberts?" Greta asked.

"*Der Struwwelpeter* means 'Slovenly Peter.'"

"What is slovenly?" asked Greta.

"That means someone who is not very clean or neat about his appearance," Jason clarified.

"Oh, you mean a bum, like Luke, who used to come into the store?"

"That's right," replied Mr. Roberts. Now here is the story."

By the time Mr. Roberts reached the middle of the story, Sven had moved over to his other side so he could see better. Even Jason was drawn to the reading of the picture book.

See this frowsy "cratur"
Pah! It's Struwwelpeter!
On his fingers rusty,
On his tow-head musty,
Scissors seldom come;
Let his talons grow a year,
Hardly ever combs his hair,
Do any loathe him? Some!
They hail him "Modern satyre—
Disgusting Struwwelpeter."

By the end of the story, Sven had climbed up into Mr. Robert's lap, so he could look at the pictures better. Jason and Greta just shook their heads in amazement. Jason said in a hushed tone to Greta, "Wonders never cease."

Later that same day, Long John came by the store for the kids to take them fishing. "Have either of you children been fishing before?" he asked.

"No," responded Greta.

"So, I don't suppose you have fishing poles, either."

"No."

"That's okay. We can make poles out of bamboo. I know where some bamboo is growing. Follow me."

He headed toward Chin Lee's house. When he arrived there, Chin Lee was busy hanging out the latest batch of laundry.

"Hey, Chin Lee, we need some bamboo for fishing poles. Do you mind if we cut some of the bamboo you have growing out back?"

"You cut what you need, but don't hurt small bamboo sprouts. Chin Lee need them for cooking."

"So, that's what these funny-looking trees are," remarked Greta.

Long John showed them how the bamboo grew in long, sealed, hollow chambers that made the pole strong but flexible. He led them lower down on Wolf Creek and showed them how to rig a line and hook on the end of their bamboo poles. While they were fishing, Greta asked Long John, "You have a funny name. Why do they call you Long John?"

"Now, that's a funny story. My name is really John Long. But I happen to wear a pair of long johns when I sleep—you know, the red flannel kind, with a trap door in the back."

Greta and Sven both giggled at the picture he created in their minds.

"One night, before you came to Grass Valley—it was called Boston Ravine back then—there was a fire. I ran out to help with the fire brigade, but I didn't take the time to put on my britches. After the fire was all out, there I was, standing around in my red, flannel long johns, and someone made the wise crack that I should be called Long John instead of John Long. And the name stuck."

The leaves of some of the oak trees along Wolf Creek were falling off in the cool, autumn weather. Long John and the kids could hear the squirrels chucking in the oak trees as they gathered acorns for their winter. Overhead, they heard the honking of geese heading south for the winter.

Long John and the children hadn't been fishing in the creek long when an eager young lad of about nineteen years rode up on a horse with a distinctive spot on its hind quarter. "Is this Grass Valley?" he asked Long John.

"Yup, you've found Grass Valley."

'I'm looking for a man named Jason Miller. Do you know where his claim is?"

"Why are you looking for him? What's your name, Young Fella?" Long John asked with suspicion.

"I'm Bill Dedmore."

"Any relation to Elizabeth Dedmore from Davenport, Iowa?"

"Yes, as a matter of fact; she's my sister. So, you do know Jason?"

"Try the general store. It's located further up this creek, just beyond that low hill there."

###

A little puzzled why he was being directed to a general store, Bill was nonetheless anxious to make contact with Jason. But instead of heading in the direction Long John indicated, he turned back the way he had come and raced to the remains of the wagon train waiting a short distance away.

Elizabeth asked, "Are we lost? I told you, Joseph Walker should have come with us all the way to Grass Valley."

Joseph Walker was no longer with the train. After putting those few wagons going all the way to Grass Valley on the trail heading from San Francisco to Grass Valley, he had placed Bill in charge before he'd headed up the coast to his land in Contra Costa. John Riker had left the remains of the train to Joseph Walker when he reached his home in Lompoc before they had even arrived in San Francisco.

"I've found someone who knows Jason. Follow me," he directed Elizabeth.

Jason stood absently dusting a display of dry goods while he worried if Elizabeth would accept his missing arm, and he also fretted over just where they were on their journey west. Two people rushed by him as they entered the store.

"Can I help you folks?"

Elizabeth, recognizing Jason's voice, turned and immediately ran into his arms.

"Elizabeth! You finally made it. I can't believe it. You're here at last."

"Oh, my darling Jason, it's been so long since I last saw you." They stepped back to get better looks at each other. She had noticed something strange about his hug. She took hold of his fake right hand and gasped in surprise.

"Oh, my goodness! What happened to you?"

Jason was somewhat reluctant to bring up his disability so soon, but what else could he do? "Well, you see, back in June, about the time you started west on the wagon train, there was a mine cave-in. And I got injured in the rescue attempt. I lost my right hand and arm up to here." He pulled up his sleeve to show where his fake, wooden arm was joined—what was left of his real arm. He heard another gasp from Elizabeth and looked deep into her eyes to gauge her reaction.

He was surprised not to see horror or rejection in her gaze. Instead, he saw the same compassion and love he had seen when he first proposed to her back in Davenport, Iowa. For the first time since his accident, Jason had renewed faith and hope in his engagement to Elizabeth.

Bill, who had been hanging back so as to give his sister and Jason an opportunity to have their own reunion, took this time to step forward and greet Jason. Jason focused on Bill for the first time and said, "Well, who is this? It can't be your little brother, Billy. Why, you've grown up and become a man."

Bill laughed and embraced Jason with an exuberant, back-slapping hug.

They were interrupted by Esther, who entered the store in search of Elizabeth and Bill.

"Jason, this is Esther Sterling," introduced Elizabeth. "She is an orphan I've adopted from the wagon train."

Esther stepped up and took Elizabeth's hand. She was a little hesitant but finally said, "This is my new mommy."

"Well, well, well! Isn't that a coincidence? I have kind of inherited two orphans of my own," Jason responded.

At that point, Long John, with his two charges, walked into the store.

"And here they are now. Greta and Sven, this is my fiancée, Elizabeth, and her brother, Bill, I've told you so much about. They've just arrived here from Iowa."

Elizabeth was flabbergasted at first but quickly recovered and said, "Well, I do declare, I've got my two fondest wishes—soon I'll have my very own family and a class to teach. And it looks like my class will be in my home. We do have a home, don't we, Jason?"

Jason was standing close beside Elizabeth, and he tentatively reached for her hand, making sure he was using his good hand. Elizabeth smiled over at him and grasped it eagerly.

Smiling down at her, he responded, "We not only have a home, but we also have a general store and a mining claim, in case anyone wants to work it for me."

"I will!" Bill raised his hand as everyone laughed.

Next, Susan walked in with her parents, and Bill immediately put his arm about her and introduced them to everyone. He started with, "This is my new bride, Susan; we just got married in Santa Cruz. And here are Susan's parents, Bart and Joanna Smith."

Jason felt a big weight lifted from his heart. He said a prayer: *Thank You, God, for bringing them all here safely.* He felt kind of like he was living his dream, but then he thought, *This is better than any dream I've had.*

###

On a crisp, fall afternoon the following week, Elizabeth was helping Jason at the general store. She saw Jason trying to move a heavy box of mining equipment up to a high shelf. She quickly ran over and said, "Jason, let me help with that."

Jason stopped and looked at her strangely. "That's okay, Lizzy. I should have used my lifting apparatus that I rigged up." He went to the back room and came out, pulling a complicated-looking contraption onto which he moved the heavy box. Then with his one good hand, he pulled on a series of ropes and pulleys that moved the box up to the shelf with ease.

"Wow, that's ingenious, Jason! I can see you have adjusted to having only one hand. I'll not make that mistake again."

Elizabeth had told Jason about her abduction on the trip west, but she hadn't told him about Dr. Freeman's warning that she might not be able to have babies. She knew she had to tell him because she knew he wanted a big family, and she'd been trying to get up the nerve to do so. She turned to him and taking both of his hands in hers, said, "I have something important to tell you, Jason."

Jason gazed into her beautiful, blue eyes and seeing how serious she was, said, "What is it, Lizzy?"

"Remember about me being abducted by Chief Tishomingo and falling off my horse when he escaped? Well . . . " She hesitated, then went on. "Doc Freeman said I might not be able to have babies after my injury."

Jason absorbed what she had told him for a moment, then responded, "Wow, Lizzy, isn't three children enough—to start with, anyway?" Tears sprung to her eyes in relief, and she gripped his hands tighter. He continued, "We can always adopt additional children in the future, you know. Would that satisfy you?"

She pulled him into her arms and hugged him tight, then murmured, "I love you so much, Jason. That would be wonderful."

Jason felt at peace at last with his greatest worries put to rest and the woman he loved in his arms.

###

A week had passed since Elizabeth and Bill had arrived in Grass Valley. Jason was ready to get married. He said to Long John, "I remember you told me you used to be a preacher. Is there any chance that you still have the authority to marry us?"

Long John looked into it and had found out he was still an ordained preacher and could legally perform marriages, even in California.

Elizabeth had had the foresight and, thanks to her thrifty nature, had saved enough money to buy a wedding gown while in San Francisco. She was all decked out in her two-piece Victorian wedding dress with detachable under sleeves. The bodice was boned, double-lined, with piping in most seams. It had a handstitched, gathered front panel and a hand-finished bottom bodice trim. The closure was in back, fastened with hidden buttons and buttonholes. She had a fully lined skirt with four ruffled tiers attached to an outer skirt. This gown was made of batiste cotton-lined and trimmed with satin ribbon.

Susan, Elizabeth's matron of honor, was finishing buttoning the gown up the back. "Are you nervous?" she asked Elizabeth.

"No . . . well, maybe a little," she replied.

"Jason seems to be a real catch with his general store and all. He's a handsome man."

"Yes, I love him dearly."

"The ready-made family doesn't bother you?"

"No, not at all. It just gives us a head start. I always wanted a big family of my own."

"Well, you two certainly have a head start on that," Susan remarked. "God works in mysterious ways."

Meanwhile, Jason waited nervously with Long John for his bride to appear. "Is it proper for you to be both the best man and the preacher?" he asked.

Long John laughed and said, "I've never heard of it happening before, but there is no law I know of agin it."

Jason was sporting a new suit he had purchased in Sacramento. He had shaved off his miner's beard and had gotten a fresh haircut.

Suddenly, the band, made up of Jason's miner friends, struck up a loud, rough tune. Jason and Long John cringed at first. But then, they looked at each other with grins, and Jason shrugged, as if to say, *What did you expect from this bunch of rowdy miners?*

They turned, and Jason saw Susan first, then Elizabeth starting up the rose petal-strewn aisle of the Nevada City Methodist Church, where they chose to have their ceremony. The church was first built in 1850 by the pioneer preacher Reverend Isaac Owen on a different site but moved to the present side on Broad Street last year in 1852. This was one of the few churches built in the goldfield.

Jason was stunned by the beautiful woman floating down the aisle toward him. Her radiant smile erased any lingering doubts that he had over whether Elizabeth still wanted to marry him.

The smile never left her face as she purposely broke tradition and stood to Jason's right and took Jason's fake wooden right hand in her left hand.

Jason returned her smile, basking in the glow of the moment. He barely heard Long John as he said, "Dearly beloved, we are gathered here . . . "

He finally came out of his trance when Long John asked the question, "Do you, Jason, take Elizabeth to be your wife, to love, cherish, and protect for as long as you both shall live?"

"I do," he said.

"Elizabeth, do you take Jason to be your husband, to love, honor, obey, and cherish for as long as you both shall live?"

"I do," she said.

"I now pronounce you man and wife. Jason, you may kiss your bride."

Jason took Elizabeth into his arms and tenderly kissed her amidst the applause, cat calls, and whistles from the assembled family and miner friends.

"And now, I introduce to you Mr. and Mrs. Jason Miller."

They turned and walked down the aisle hand-in-hand into their future together, in the land of golden opportunities.

"Do we have a place to celebrate?" Elizabeth asked her new husband.

"We sure do, Lizzy! I have our wedding trip all worked out. We have reservations at the Exchange Hotel for the weekend. It's right here in Grass Valley. And I will just have to close the store while we are gone."

###

Later at dinner in the restaurant of the Exchange Hotel, Elizabeth patted her full stomach and looked about at the other diners. "I swear I've seen that guy somewhere before," she commented in a low tone to Jason.

Turning, Jason replied, "You mean that guy at the second table over with the bushy hair and mustache?"

"Yes, he's very familiar."

"Maybe you met him on your journey west."

"Shhh, he's coming this way."

Stopping at the newlyweds' table, the gentleman doffed his hat and addressed Elizabeth. "I believe we have met before. I never forget a face, especially one as pretty as yours, ma'am. I'm Samuel Clemens."

"Oh, yes, I remember you. Did you quit your job on the riverboat?

"Why, yes, I decided to come west. I got here so fast by taking the stagecoach. I'm in the process of writing a story about that adventure."

"Of course, you're a writer as well as a storyteller. Jason, where are my manners? Mr. Samuel Clemens, this is my husband, Jason Miller. We met Mr. Clemens on the riverboat at the start of our journey west."

"Very pleased to meet you, sir."

"You must be the miner this lovely young lady was pining for. Have you struck it rich in the goldfield?"

"Yes, I have certainly struck it rich, but not by finding gold. Elizabeth and I were married yesterday. She is the gold that every miner in this goldfield dreams of but rarely finds."

Chapter Sixteen

ALL'S WELL THAT ENDS WELL

GRASS VALLEY GOLDFIELD

NOVEMBER 2, 1854

(ONE YEAR LATER)

Jason walked in the door of his brand-new home on Gold Hill. His general store was booming, and he had designed and built the new home with many bedrooms and lots of room for his large family.

"Where is your mother?" Jason asked Greta, who came out to greet her dad in the hall.

"She's feeling a little poorly and went to her room to rest."

Esther and Sven ran through the hall, hand in hand, singing a silly song they had made up recently about Struwwelpeter.

Jason took the time to chase them down and swooped them up, one by one, with his good arm, and swung them around the expansive living room. They both squealed in glee and hugged their father.

He put them down after a few moments and headed toward his and Elizabeth's bedroom, a little concerned about his wife.

When he opened the door, he almost ran into Susan, who was exiting the room. Elizabeth was saying, "Thanks for taking over my class today."

Susan had a big grin on her face, and she winked at Jason as she left. She turned back at the last moment and said, "By the way, Bill just struck it rich with his new claim!"

Jason said, "That's great!" Then, he soon forgot about it when he saw Elizabeth on her hands and knees vomiting into a bedpan.

"Darling, what's wrong?" he asked, concern coloring his request.

"I'm feeling a little queasy" was her reply as she held her long, brown hair back from her face.

Jason helped her back to her feet and walked her to the bed, where she sank down, grateful for his help.

"How long has this been going on?" Jason asked in an anxious voice.

"Not long," she replied. After a moment, she smiled and said, "Well, it looks like old Doc Freeman was wrong with his diagnosis."

It took a moment, but then Jason came to the realization of what Elizabeth was talking about. "You mean . . . " he started.

"Yes, darling, I think I'm going to have a baby."

Jason enveloped Elizabeth in a crushing hug.

"Careful, darling," Elizabeth protested with tears of joy in her eyes. "You are hugging more than just me here."

"I'll call Marcos to come by and take a look at you first thing tomorrow," Jason told her.

They both couldn't believe this unexpected development.

Jason knelt down beside the bed, took Elizabeth's hand, and prayed, "Thank You, Lord, for answering our prayers."

Elizabeth added, "Amen."

THE END

SOURCES FOR THE WRITING OF *SIERRA GOLD FEVER*

Alexander, Kathy Weiser. "Bloody Island Massacre, California." Legends of America. December, 2017. https://www.legendsofamerica.com/bloody-island-massacre.

Brown, Juanita Kennedy. *Nuggets of California History 5th Ed.* Nevada City: Nevada County Historical Society, 1990.

Calhoon, F. D. *California Gold and the Highgraders, True Stories of the Mines and Miners.* Cal-Con Press, 1988.

"California Missions, The." California Missions Foundation. Accessed November 25, 2021. http://californiamissionsfoundation.org/the-california-missions.

"Captain Weimar." North Fork Trails. April 4, 2006. www.northforktrails.blogspot.com/2006/04/captain-weimar.html.

"Calvary Out Posts of the 1st Calvary Division and Subordinate Commands." 1996. http://www.first-team.us.

Chalmers, Claudine. *Grass Valley, Image of America.* Mount Pleasant: Arcadia Publishing, 2006.

Comstock, David A. *Gold Diggers and Camp Followers, 1845-1851*. Nevada City: Comstock Bonanza Press, 1988.

Flint, Richard and Shirley. "Cimarron Cutoff to the Santa Fe Trail." New Mexico State Records Center & Archives. Accessed February 25, 2018. http://newmexicohistory.org/places/cimarron-cutoff-of-the-santa-fe-trail.

Historical Overview: (A Brief History of the Panama Railroad) Part III." Panama Railroad.org. Accessed December 2, 2021. www.panamarailroad.org/historyc.htm.

"Indian Removal Act." HistoryNet. Accessed February 25, 2018. http://www.historynet.com/indian-removal-act.

Koeppel, Elliot H. *The California Goldfield: Highway 49 Revisited*. 2nd ed. Pine Grove: Cenotto Publishers, 1999.

Malloy, Betsy. "History and Guide to Mission Santa Cruz." TripSavvy.com. August 16, 2019. https://www.tripsavvy.com/mission-santa-cruz-1478426?utm_term=mission%2Bsanta%2Bcruz%2Bfacts&utm_content=p1-main-1-title&utm_medium=sem&utm_source=msn_s&utm_campaign=adid-c0dccd0b-e166-4dac-b753-ee9c0594da03-0-ab_msb_ocode-603409&ad=semD&an=msn_s&am=broad&q=mission%2Bsanta%2Bcruz%2Bfacts&o=603409&qsrc=999&l=sem&askid=c0dccd0b-e166-4dac-b753-ee9c0594da03-0-ab_msb.

McQuiston, F.W. Jr. *Gold: The Saga of the Empire Mine 1850-1956*. 2nd ed. Nevada City: Blue Dolphin Publishers, 2012.

Peters, Arthur King. *Seven Trails West*. New York: Abbeville Press, 2000.

Ruhlen, Col. George. "Fort Rosecrans," Military Museum.org. February 10, 2000. http://www.militarymuseum.org/FtRosecrans.html.

Stammerjohn, George. "The Mythical Fort Tejon 'Camel Corps." The Fort Tejon Historical Association. Accessed February 25, 2018. http://forttejon.org/camel.html.

Steen, Francis F. "A Short Story of Los Angles." UCLA.edu. Accessed February 25, 2018. http://cogweb.ucla.edu/Chumash/LosAngeles.html.

Trimble, Marshall. "Joe Walker Mountain Man, Scout and Explorer." *True West Magazine* online. October 18, 2016. https://truewestmagazine. com/joe-walker-mountain-man-scout-and-explorer.

Turbine, Francis. TurbineGenerator. Accessed February 25, 2018. https://www.turbinegenerator.org/hydro/hydropower-types/ francis-turbine.

Twain, Mark (Samuel Clemens). *Life on the Mississippi, Complete.* The Project Gutenberg eBook of Life on The Mississippi. August 20, 2006. http://www.gutenberg.org/files/245/245-h/245-h.htm#linkc58.

Twain, Mark. "Dick Baker's Cat." In *Lords of the Housetops: Thirteen Cat Tales.* Carl Van Vechten, ed. 1921. https://americanliterature. com/author/mark-twain/short-story/dick-bakers-cat.

For more information about
D. Michael O'Haver
and
Sierra Gold Fever
please visit:

ohavers-lighthouse-beacon-press.square.site

Ambassador International's mission is to magnify the Lord Jesus Christ and promote His Gospel through the written word.

We believe through the publication of Christian literature, Jesus Christ and His Word will be exalted, believers will be strengthened in their walk with Him, and the lost will be directed to Jesus Christ as the only way of salvation.

For more information about
AMBASSADOR INTERNATIONAL
please visit:

www.ambassador-international.com
@AmbassadorIntl
www.facebook.com/AmbassadorIntl

Thank you for reading this book. Please consider leaving us a review on your favorite retailer's website, Goodreads or Bookbub, or our website.

More from Ambassador International

Sarah Bakker has spent years getting over her love for Michael Thomas. After he went MIA, Sarah thought her heart would never heal. But when he is found alive and returns home, Sarah is thrown together with him to prepare for the town's annual Christmas pageant. Perhaps Sarah will finally find the love she longs for—even if it's only in her dreams.

King Solomon is well-known as a wise man and the wealthiest king to have ever lived. But with great power often comes great corruption, and Solomon was no exception—including his collection of wives and concubines. But who were these women? What was life like for them in Solomon's harem? S.A. Jewell dives into a deeper part of Solomon's kingdom and shows how God is always faithful, even when we may doubt His plan.

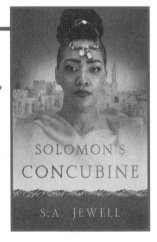

After Catherine Reed's husband dies, she moves back home in order to accept a new position as the teacher for the town's one-room schoolhouse. Samuel Harris has suffered his own loss and guilt has burdened him ever since. When his old flame comes back to town, he wonders if they can find healing together . . .

Made in the USA
Columbia, SC
26 July 2024